BEHIND CLOSED DOORS

ELIZABETH WOOLLEY

BEHIND CLOSED DOORS

By Elizabeth Woolley

BEHIND CLOSED DOORS

By Elizabeth Woolley

Copyright Elizabeth Woolley 2020

Cover Art by Elizabeth Woolley
Editing by Elizabeth Woolley
Formatting by Elizabeth Woolley
Published by Elizabeth Woolley

Dedicated to my family and friends, both online and in real life, without whom the last few years would have been infinitely harder. Love to you all.

❀ Created with Vellum

BEHIND CLOSED DOORS

CHAPTER 1

$\mathcal{G}$RACE BENNETT

GRACE BENNETT, the Vicar of Saint Saviour's Church in Swinbury in Oxfordshire, England, smiled and nodded as she stood at the church door, bidding her congregation farewell, after her regular Sunday service. As she was passed by the usual mixture of familiar faces, she reflected on the words of the Bishop, when he had recommended this job to her, as being a calm, peaceful backwater; a place to heal after the trauma of what had happened to her in Liverpool. Hmmm. Appearances can be deceiving. Sometimes there is more going on behind closed doors than we can ever imagine.

CHARLOTTE TRENT & DENNIS MASON

. . .

CHARLOTTE TRENT WAS A PRETTY CHILD; the sort of child that adults wanted to coo over—with naturally blonde curls and blue eyes and a dimple in her chin. She was the adored only child of Doreen Trent. She was, it seemed, destined for a charmed life; a life she came close to losing at the age of five, when she evaded her mother's grasp and ran into the road, as they queued at the bakery.

For many years Doreen told the tale to friends and strangers alike, about how she came close to losing her darling daughter. Many had heard the story before, but they indulged Doreen over what had clearly been a traumatic event in her life. Some told their own children the tale, as a warning of what might happen if they behaved in a similar fashion.

"Mum, do you have to...?" Charlotte sighed as her mother repeated the tale at the parents' evening of Westlands High School, to Miss Lake, her English teacher, as they discussed Charlotte's term performance. She was a bright child and rarely gave her parents or teachers cause for concern over her grades. Miss Lake smiled sympathetically at Charlotte, but wanted to tell her to appreciate her mother's concern. If only she had a mother who was as loving and concerned as Doreen. Her own mother was, quite frankly, a battle axe, and meeting some of the parents at such events made her sigh with envy.

Charlotte's attention was distracted by the handsome figure of Dennis Mason, who was in a separate queue with his father, to discuss his poor maths performance that term. He caught her gaze and smiled at her. Everyone smiled at

Charlotte. It was hard not to smile. She was one of those people who collected smiles and people often smiled involuntarily at the pretty young girl, whether they were deserved or not.

Dennis winked at her and made a rude gesture behind his father's back, mimicking with his hand that he was talking too much. She laughed. She must "accidentally" run into him in the corridor some time, and maybe he would ask her out. She was fifteen, and her mother, being protective, told her that she wouldn't allow her to go on dates until she was sixteen.

"There's plenty of time for boys when you get older, my girl. You just concentrate on passing your exams, and getting that job you're after in Sensations."

Sensations was a beauty parlour that had opened on the High Street the previous summer. To both Doreen and her daughter, the place was the height of sophistication and a very desirable place to work for a pretty young girl like Charlotte. After all, Doreen didn't expect her daughter to have to work many years, before a handsome man would whisk her off to the smart new housing estate at the edge of town, where expensive cars sat on the drives, and elegant and pampered women would wait to allow their husbands to run around the vehicle to open the door for their wives. That was the way that be-suited executives treated the women in their lives, thought Doreen, who had never had the car door opened for her in her life. Her former husband, Charlotte's father was, quite frankly, an uncouth brute, who burped at the table, and talked in grunts. It had been a relief when he had walked out on the family when Charlotte was just eight years old. She definitely wanted something different for her daughter.

In another queue, Doreen spotted the sickly child, Elizabeth Cook, in her wheelchair, being pushed by her father. She couldn't help but feel sorry for a child such as her, but thanked her lucky stars that her own daughter was so healthy and pretty by comparison. Elizabeth was a year younger than Charlotte, but looked small enough to be several years below her. Apparently, she had cystic fibrosis, Doreen had heard, which had seriously affected her lungs, and she frequently had to depend on an oxygen cylinder to assist with her breathing. Her father had to massage her chest every day, Doreen had learned, to enable his daughter to clear the mucus that clogged up her airways. She turned away from the girl. It didn't seem right to stare at her, poor thing.

IT WAS two days later when the first opportunity arose for Charlotte to "accidentally" run into Dennis Mason at school. She spotted him walking towards her, and he was alone for a change. He was a popular boy and usually accompanied by two or three of his friends. As he arrived within a few feet of her, she casually dropped her history book on to the floor. Dennis, being polite and well-mannered, immediately bent and picked up the book, handing it back to Charlotte with a smile.

"Thanks very much. Trying to carry too many books at once."

Actually, she only had four books, and both of them knew that this was a contrived excuse.

"That's okay. Glad I could help."

He would have then moved on, but Charlotte gave him such a glorious smile, he was temporarily overwhelmed—which was her intention.

"It's so nice to meet a gentleman. My mother says they are a dying breed."

Dennis looked a little uncomfortable. At sixteen he was already gaining the height and stature of an adult male, but in his mind, he often felt more like a twelve-year-old schoolboy when in the presence of a girl like Charlotte. Yes, he could flirt from a distance, or if in a group with his mates. But he hadn't quite grasped the casual stance and language of a young stud. However, he had a natural charm and was blessed with a pleasing face and body. He would probably never have to try too hard to capture a girl's heart.

Charlotte was about to move off, but paused, giving him every opportunity to make a move. He took the plunge just as she was about to leave.

"Would you like to go for a walk after school—perhaps along the canal path? It's nice down there at this time of year."

Charlotte smiled, and waited the requisite five seconds, so as to not look over eager.

"Yes, I'd like that. I'll meet you at the school gate, shall I?"

AND SO THEIR RELATIONSHIP BEGAN—CLANDESTINELY at first, because of Doreen's possible displeasure. Charlotte suspected that her mother would like Dennis. After all, he was polite, handsome, and bright. What he lacked, however, was age and earning power. His father owned a small building and decorating business, and Dennis had plans to join him in the business after school. He had prospects, therefore, thought Charlotte. She was sure that her mother would come to like Dennis when she met him, and looked forward to her sixteenth birthday, when she planned to ask permission to go on her first proper date.

In the meantime, she and Dennis began meeting whenever they could. They held hands as they walked on the country footpaths in the neighbourhood, and kissed on the lips whenever they parted. Dennis longed to become more intimate with her, but he was wise enough to know that here was a girl who wouldn't be happy with a fumble from his fingers behind the bike shed at school. Within weeks of meeting her, he realised that Charlotte was a girl with whom he could make a future.

Finally, her sixteenth birthday arrived, and Charlotte revealed her secret to her mother. Doreen had been annoyed at first that her daughter had been seeing this boy behind her back, and demanded that she invite him home for tea before she would consent to her precious girl being perhaps sullied by someone unsuitable. Her hope was, in fact, that the relationship, her daughter's first romance, would eventually fizzle out, for she was much too young to be serious with anyone.

When the meeting took place, Doreen was pleasantly surprised by this handsome young man, with impeccable manners, and consented for Charlotte to accompany him to the cinema the following Friday.

"But you're to come straight home after the film is over," she told them. "No loitering around."

It was loitering that had led to her being caught up with

Charlotte's Dad, and look what a boorish, no-hoper he had turned out to be.

The film wasn't that exciting, and when Dennis suggested they leave half way through, Charlotte was happy to do so. This extra time meant they were able to do a little canoodling in the alleyway behind the Regal cinema, even though Charlotte was firm in what he was allowed and not allowed to do with his hands. She remembered the words her mother had used, when they had "the talk".

"A man won't want the Christmas present if he's already unwrapped the paper," was one of the strange analogies she used. Charlotte wasn't entirely in agreement with that, but understood what her mother was trying to say. But as the months went on, and the couple became more attracted to each other, it became harder to remain as chaste as Doreen hoped for her daughter. Slowly, she allowed Dennis a little more latitude, knowing that if not, she might lose his interest if other, more easy-going girls, were to offer him tempta-tions he found hard to refuse.

When his hands crept up her jumper, towards her pert little breasts, Charlotte allowed him to touch her soft skin and massage her nipples. She found she actually enjoyed it. But she proved more resistant to his hands travelling in the opposite direction. Lying in his bed later, after taking Char-lotte home, Dennis enjoyed fantasising about what he wanted to do with her, and that satisfied him for the time being. He was sure that she would relax the rules in time.

Doreen inevitably told Dennis the story about the lucky escape from death Charlotte had, at the age of five, and why she was a little more anxious about her daughter because of it. Charlotte squirmed as she heard the story yet again, and this time to her boyfriend, but Dennis liked that her mother cared enough about her daughter's safety.

They both agreed that the summer that year was the best one they had ever had. As Charlotte edged towards her seventeenth birthday, she finally relented and let Dennis's hands discover the secret place between her thighs, that he had been longing to discover for months. It was in the tall grass of the meadow near the railway that they lay and Dennis did his exploring. Charlotte was both thrilled and afraid. Suppose her mother was right? Suppose, after she had let him explore her, he lost all respect for her. She couldn't bear the thought that he would think her the same as that tramp, Julie Rogers, who had been had by several boys, she had heard, who now mocked her to their mates. Would Dennis talk about her in the same way. She voiced her concerns.

"Of course I wouldn't, Charlotte. I respect you. I would never think of you like that."

At that moment, his fingers were poised to slide under the elastic around the legs of her knickers. He would have said anything at that point. But she recognised the honesty in his voice, and allowed him to proceed. Well, only so far, of course. She mustn't let him unwrap his Christmas present too soon, after all.

Both of them being respectfully handsome and beautiful, the attractive couple were popular at school. Younger girls looked wistfully at them, as though imagining themselves in such a place in a year or two—if they could just lose that spare tyre, or make the spots disappear—hardly acknowledging that there was more to life than being beautiful and popular. The boys hero-worshipped Dennis. They equated him with the status of a man who had it all—ignoring the fact that Dennis's academic achievements weren't very spectacular, and he was only average on the sport's field. But the fact that he could attract and keep a girl like Charlotte, placed him up on the pedestal with their other heroes.

Dennis told Charlotte that he loved her, when they had been dating for six months. She didn't respond immediately, which made him a little nervous. But she didn't seem repulsed by the thought, and he was sure she was simply playing hard to get. They kissed and "made out" all summer and he had no doubt that they would stay together, and eventually, when he was established in his father's business, she would consent to become his wife. He had no doubt about that.

They should have had a charmed life. Charlotte should have obtained a job at Sensations after leaving school, working her way, she hoped, from junior to trained beautician. She would wear the smart, pale blue uniform, and have access to unlimited hair and beauty treatments, and life would follow the plan mapped out for her so many years earlier by her mother, and which she had come to accept as being her best route to marriage to a handsome and successful businessman, who would be able to keep her in the style that both she, and her mother, had always wanted.

But life has a habit of kicking people when they least expect it. One day, when she was crossing the High Street to meet Dennis on the other side, after some Saturday shopping, the accident she had evaded at five years old came back for a second attempt. A lorry was travelling just a little too fast along the busy road, the driver anxious to deliver his goods to a shop before closing time. Charlotte's mind was on her recent purchases and on Dennis, opposite. She stepped out from behind a parked van at the exact moment that the lorry arrived. She didn't stand a chance. Her shopping was thrown up into the air, landing on the road, to be crushed by the large tyres and that was Charlotte's fate too.

Women nearby, who had seen the accident, screamed loudly. Dennis stood frozen to the spot, in complete shock, unable to comprehend what he was seeing. An ambulance arrived in minutes, as a passing policeman stopped the traffic and took control of the situation. Faces looked grim. It didn't seem likely that Charlotte would survive such an impact. It was her head that had taken most of the damage. Her torso looked almost unmarked. The policeman crossed to where Dennis was clutching the front of a parked car, and looking very pale. He was in severe shock, the policeman concluded, but he was able to give Charlotte's name and her mother's telephone number to him.

A second ambulance arrived, and it was decided that Charlotte would be taken in the first one, with Dennis following on behind.

"The lad's in shock. I think he needs checking out," said the policeman, to no one in particular, as though he had to justify his decision.

By the time Dennis arrived at the hospital, Charlotte had been taken into the operating theatre for possible surgery. It seemed she was still alive. Doreen arrived at the hospital in a police car, just ten minutes later. Her face looked completely drained of blood, and she stumbled slightly as she walked along the corridor.

Before Dennis had a chance to talk to her, a doctor came and whisked Doreen into a nearby room. It was just a minute later when Dennis heard the most chilling wail come from the room, followed by huge, wracking sobs. He prepared himself for the worst.

A nurse brought him a mug of hot, sweet tea, and tried to soothe him.

"You've had a bad shock. You need to stay for a little while until we check you out."

A doctor emerged from the room nearby and came over to Dennis.

"I understand you're Charlotte's boyfriend."

He was using the present tense. Maybe there was hope, after all. He nodded.

"Would you mind coming to be with her mother for a moment. She has had a tremendous shock, and you're the closest she has to her daughter right now. Can you just sit with her, while a nurse prepares a sedative?"

In the room, Doreen looked completely overwhelmed. She barely even acknowledged his presence. The doctor took one of her hands.

"Mrs Trent, here's Dennis. He's come to sit with you for a few minutes."

She looked up, hollow-eyed, at Dennis, and spoke for the first time.

"She's brain dead, they say."

The doctor tried to reassure her, but wasn't very good at this part of his job.

"We don't know that for sure, Mrs Trent. We need to do some tests and scan the brain, to make sure what is happening there."

. . .

DOREEN AND DENNIS stayed overnight at the hospital, and Doreen was with her daughter the following morning when the decision was made that there was no sign of significant activity in the brain and that the machine keeping her alive would be switched off. Charlotte Trent's life ended at the tender age of sixteen, and both her mother and boyfriend believed that their lives too had ended.

Before the machine was switched off, the doctors had a long talk with Doreen, about the possibility of organ transplants from her daughter.

"She can help so many people if you agree to this. Her death won't have been completely in vain. We know this is an agonizing decision to have to make at such a time, but we would be failing in our jobs if we didn't at least mention this possibility to you. After some thought, Doreen gave her assent, and eventually was taken home to grieve.

She couldn't recover from the loss of her daughter—the repository of all her hopes and dreams. She began to drink to deaden the pain, and became a recluse, only leaving the house to buy food and other essentials.

Dennis, meanwhile, coped with his grief as best he could. He left school and started work with his father. But he knew he would never forget his beautiful Charlotte.

CHAPTER 2

ORINDA LAKE

As her mother screeched at her from the other room, Dorinda gritted her teeth and supressed the urge to scream back at her. Dolores Lake had been irritable and cantankerous all her life, it seemed, but the dementia had now made her worse. She and her mother had lived together for the past eight years, since it became clear that she could no longer take care of herself because of the illness that was eating away at her brain. Dorinda had hardly known a day's peace since.

As a child, Dorinda had taken refuge in books, despite her hobby being disparaged by her mother.

"Books are a waste of time, my girl. They just give people fancy ideas. Why don't you do something useful like knitting or sewing? At least you will have something to wear at the end."

Dorinda stubbornly refused to allow her mother to spoil the enjoyment she took in the books she had once borrowed from the library, but more recently, bought for herself. She became completely engrossed in the stories, of love and romance, of adventure, of thrills and spills—she read widely and voraciously. They were her escape from her mother.

People wondered why she put up with her mother's treatment, but she thought she had probably become somewhat immune to the sound of Dolores' voice; which had changed little since she was a child. Her father, when he was alive, took refuge on his allotment, at the other side of the main road, where he spent every hour when he wasn't working as a postal worker, growing fruit and vegetables for the family. He, too, seemed deaf to the screeching sound of his ever-critical wife.

"These carrots you've brought me, they're strange shapes and have worm holes in them. Can't you grow nice straight ones like they have in the shops."

He could have responded that carrots didn't grow well in his heavy clay soil, and that he didn't use any chemicals to repel pests—but he remained silent. Dolores had her say, and he continued to read the newspaper throughout her tirade. He had his escape, however, on the day, ten years earlier, when he was found dead on the allotment, by a neighbouring gardener. His heart had stopped beating. Since then, Dorinda had to face the onslaughts from her mother alone, and was slightly annoyed that her father had left her in this situation.

.   .   .

SHE ENJOYED her teaching at Westlands High School. It seemed a place of tranquillity compared to her home. She remembered Charlotte Trent starting at the school, and envied her seemingly perfect life—having a devoted mother, a pretty face, beautiful hair, and popular with her fellow pupils, especially the boys. Dorinda had always considered herself very ordinary; not ugly, but a bit boring, with a forgettable face and slightly dumpy body. Because of her low opinion of her own attractiveness, she never bothered to dress in a way that might catch the eye of any possible boyfriend. She had had the occasional date over the years, but became tongue-tied when having a conversation with anyone, so they never amounted to anything.

In the classroom, however, she came alive. It was almost like being on the stage, and she was playing a part in a play. History was her passion, and she succeeded, despite her negative opinion of her talents, to enthuse a few of her students with her subject. She noticed that Dennis Mason, then a rather shy and gauche twelve-year-old, came alive when she talked about well-known characters from history —the gorier they were, the more Dennis's eyes lit up. She hoped he wasn't a future mass killer, hiding his tendencies beneath a quiet exterior. Charlotte, on the other hand, couldn't hide her revulsion at some of the despots of the past. There seemed a definite divide between the girls and the boys, in terms of how much emphasis she could place on the violent deeds of some of history's rogues.

It was when she reached home that the depression set in. From the moment her mother heard the door, she began ranting. Some people who knew them had suggested that it was time Dorinda considered a care home for her mother, but she was seriously doubtful if any of them would take such a difficult woman as a resident. Besides, she had an almost stubborn, masochistic streak that always ruled out that option. She couldn't explain why she felt that way. It wasn't as if her mother had suddenly turned from a charming, gentle, woman into a harridan. She had hardly changed at all—just become worse, and more vocal. So why could she not just find a place for her mother and wash her hands of her? It was a question to which she had no answer.

It was during the school holiday that Dorinda's patience finally ran out. She never understood, when trying to analyse her actions afterwards, what exactly had happened. It was as though the time just before and just after the event became a blur. She recalled deciding to cook some bubble and squeak from the leftover potatoes and cabbage of the previous day, and had taken the heavy, iron frying pan down from the shelf in the kitchen. Her mother had wandered in from the living room, her hair a little wild where she had tugged at it with her hands.

"I don't like bubble and squeak," she began, in a whining voice, when she saw what her daughter was cooking.

"You've had it before. It's only the leftovers from yesterday—potato and cabbage, and I've added some fried onion to it to add more flavour."

"I won't eat it. You can't make me eat it."

Dorinda sighed heavily, but pressed on with cooking. Her mother had two choices; to eat it or go without. She was fed up with her constantly varying demands as to what she would eat.

Dolores began ranting at her daughter, and tried to grab the frying pan from her hand. It was the next moments that disappeared from Dorinda's memory when trying to recall the events to the police. There was a scream, she remembered. The next moment she was looking down at her mother, lying on the floor, a bleeding wound on the side of her head.

For several seconds she remained stunned, unable to move. She must get help was the thought that flashed through her mind. Picking up her phone from the kitchen table, she dialled for the Emergency Services.

"Which service do you require?" came the calm voice from the other end.

"Ambulance. I need an ambulance."

"Is someone hurt?"

"Yes, my mother. She's lying on the kitchen floor. She's unconscious, I think."

"Can you tell if she's breathing?"

Dorinda looked down at the motionless woman at her feet. There was no sign of her chest rising up and down, to indicate breathing.

"I don't think so. I'm not sure. Can you send help?"

The operator continued talking in her well-trained, calm voice. She dealt with events like this all the time. People panicked. It was her job to keep them calm.

"The ambulance is just a few minutes away. Go and open the door for them. Then come back to your mother, and I will tell you what to do."

Dorinda opened the front door, and could already hear the siren of the ambulance several streets away. Within two minutes both the ambulance and a police car were parked outside the house. Curious neighbours peered through their lace curtains, but no one knew them well enough to come to see if any help was required. The nearby neighbours had heard Dolores shrill voice endlessly over the past few years. Perhaps they would all get a bit of peace and quiet, if something had happened to her.

Dorinda, meanwhile, sat at the kitchen table, barely comprehending what was happening around her. She had the ridiculous thought that she had some history homework to mark that evening, and wished her mother would simply sit up and tell everyone to go away, so they could have supper and she could get on with her marking. But her mother's eyes remained resolutely closed.

The paramedics undertook their routine tests, but it seemed obvious to all present that Dolores was dead. It seemed likely that a post-mortem would be required, so the Police Surgeon, who acted for the police in such circumstances, was sent for. He would need to pronounce her dead and arrange for the body to be conducted away for a post-mortem to be carried out. The two police officers, meanwhile, were looking around the kitchen and making a mental note of what they saw. They decided to take Dorinda into the living room next door to ask her some questions, but not before one of them had been on his phone to police headquarters, to ask for the Scenes of Crime experts to come and cast their expert eyes over the room, before anything was touched or moved.

Dorinda sat on the sofa in the other room, not daring to sit in the armchair recently vacated by her mother, and was a little disturbed when one of the police officers took that seat instead. Her mother was very particular about allowing anyone to take her chosen chair.

"That chair is my mother's," she said, in a nervous whisper, as though expecting her mother to walk through the door and rant at the current occupant. The police officer simply gave her a blank look, unable to comprehend her concern.

The second officer sat on the sofa next to her, and took out his notebook from his uniform pocket. They began gently probing Dorinda about events that evening.

"You say you were cooking dinner?"

Dorinda's voice was quiet, but unhesitating.

"Yes, I was frying up the leftover vegetables to have with some meat from yesterday."

"At what point did your mother enter the kitchen?"

"I had just started to fry the vegetables together. She said she didn't like bubble and squeak."

"Was she annoyed about it?"

"No more than usual. She has dementia. But she's eaten bubble and squeak before."

"What happened next?"

Dorinda paused for a few seconds, trying to remember events of just a short while ago.

"I can't remember. Everything went blank in my memory until I saw her lying on the floor."

"Did she clutch her chest? Or perhaps make a sound?"

"I...I don't think so. I can't remember."

"Were you angry with your mother?"

Dorinda looked bleakly at the young police officer.

"I've been angry with my mother my entire life."

The two policemen looked at each other, and the one holding the notebook wrote something into it.

Their conversation was interrupted by the sound of the doorbell. It was the Police Surgeon. One of the policemen went out into the hallway to let him in, and Dorinda could hear voices and footsteps as they made their way into the kitchen. It didn't take long for him to pronounce Dolores dead, which meant the paramedics could leave. Their role had now been replaced by the undertakers, who would transport the body for the post-mortem.

The doctor remained in the kitchen for a few more minutes, before he and the police officer returned to the living room. He addressed Dorinda.

"I'm very sorry, my dear, but your mother is dead. There is nothing we can do for her. She has sustained a heavy blow to the head, which appears to have caused severe brain damage. How are you feeling? Perhaps the police officers can make you a cup of sweet tea. It helps with the shock."

He stopped talking to Dorinda, not wishing to get into conversation with her. It was up to the police to question her about events that evening. He had his own theory, but it wasn't up to him to conjecture at this point. He would simply make his report in due course. Then the matter was up to the police as to whether a crime had been committed.

He turned to the police officers.

"I take it the undertakers and Scenes of Crime have been informed?"

"Yes, doctor. They will be here shortly. When they arrive, we'll be free to leave with the lady, for the police station."

That was the first that Dorinda had heard about her being taken somewhere. But she didn't react. She still seemed to be in shock. The doctor responded to the policeman.

"Right. I'll meet you there, then. I'll need to examine the

lady before you question her, to make sure she's in a fit state for that."

BY THE FOLLOWING DAY, following their interview with Dorinda, and with the information provided by the other agencies involved, Dorinda Lake was charged with the murder of her mother Dolores, with a fall-back charge of manslaughter. It seemed clear to everyone that the cause of death was a blow to the head with the iron frying pan, and that the blow had been administered by her daughter. Gathering evidence and statements from the neighbours, it seemed to the detective assigned to the case, that Dorinda had probably been sorely pushed into this action, but if everyone murdered one of their parents after neglect or abuse, then there would be a lot of dead bodies about. But as the son of a heavy-handed father, he had a sneaking sympathy for the quiet school teacher.

Dorinda was held in custody until the case came to court, some four months later, and, by a stroke of luck, drew a sympathetic barrister, who was gifted with language, and managed to convince the jury that Dorinda was a victim too. He was also able to have Dorinda's statement about being angry with her mother struck out, as she hadn't yet been warned about her words being recorded, or yet seen a solicitor. The jury threw out the murder charge, and convicted on the manslaughter charge. In the pre-sentencing statement, the barrister convinced the judge that Dorinda was not a habitual murderer, and was unlikely to reoffend—and had killed her mother while the balance of her mind was disturbed. The judge agreed, and she was jailed for just three years. With good behaviour, she could expect to be out in less than two years.

So IT WAS, some twenty months later, that Dorinda returned to her home, a free woman. It felt strange to enter the house and not hear her mother's shrill voice. She had acknowledged to the Probation Officer that she thought she must have killed her mother, even though she could not remember doing so, and that, if so, then she was suitably remorseful for it. She had, of course, been sacked from her teaching post, which caused her immense pain. It was a career she had loved. However, to have her freedom back was of great solace. She would find something else to do with her life.

For a few months she lived quietly; barely seeing a soul. She read lots of books, listened to music and pottered around in the kitchen. Her income was meagre, but she had savings, which would help fill the gap before she could claim her pension. She wondered if she could do some private tuition; but wasn't sure what parent would want their child tutored by a convicted killer.

One morning, seeing a cream envelope on the mat, which bore the name of a firm of solicitors, embossed on the back, she was surprised to find that she was the beneficiary of a sum of money—fifty thousand pounds, in fact—left to her in the will of her late father's sister; a woman she had never met. The news was, quite frankly, shocking. No one had ever given her anything in her life, apart from a few uninspiring Christmas presents when she was younger. These had died out as her mother's dementia developed. In fact, she hadn't celebrated Christmas for many years. She didn't properly believe the bequest until the funds had been safely lodged in her bank account.

She lay in bed that night wondering what to do with the money. Obviously, she would save some of it for a rainy day, but she overwhelmingly wanted something good to be excited about. The house was in poor condition and neglected after her enforced absence. Why didn't she smarten it up? Especially the kitchen, where she spent much of her time. But who to approach? She had no idea which tradesperson to use, until the woman at the Post Office recommended a man called Arthur Mason, and gave her his number.

Arthur Mason was a fifty-five-year-old widower, and father to Dennis, whom, he informed Dorinda, was one of her former pupils.

"Of course; Dennis. I remember him. He was good at History, my subject. A very pleasant young man. How is he doing?"

"Not so good at the moment. His girlfriend, Charlotte Trent was killed in a road accident two years ago. He took it very hard. I'm trying hard to pull him out of his depression."

Dorinda was shocked at the news.

"Oh no, how tragic. Charlotte was one of my pupils too. I'm so sorry to hear that."

She didn't say why she hadn't heard the news, but they both knew where she had been when it happened. Arthur believed that discretion was called for, in the case of a potential customer. They agreed that he would come to the house to discuss the work that Dorinda required.

Arthur spent an hour and a half with Dorinda, and jotted

down her requirements in his notebook; taking the relevant measurements.

"I can get back to you with a quote in a few days, Miss Lake."

They shook hands and he left, leaving Dorinda ruminating about poor Charlotte and Dennis. There was a couple who seemed to have a charmed existence and a promising future. Life was just so unexpected at times.

ARTHUR MASON

ARTHUR MASON WAS THINKING FORWARD to his retirement. He hadn't put too much pressure on his son about joining him in the business, especially after the painful time with him losing his girlfriend in such a tragic manner. To be honest, if Dennis didn't come into the business, it was hard to think of what job he could do. He was pleasant and got along with people, which was a valuable trait to have when running a business like his, but with the best will in the world, he couldn't describe his son as clever. But he was diligent, and not clumsy, and with training from him, he was sure that he could set him up in the business well enough to run it after he retired. Perhaps if he won the contract for the work with Dorinda Lake, he might come along with him to begin learning the ropes. He set-to that night, preparing a quote, which he duly delivered the following day. Dorinda seemed pleased to see him so soon, and assured him she would be in touch as soon as she had studied his figures. She didn't say whether anyone else had been asked to tender a quote, and Arthur didn't mention it.

Despite the fact that he knew what had happened to Dorinda's mother, he felt a little sorry for her. She seemed lonely and careworn, as though she carried the weight of the world on her shoulders. He hadn't known her very well before the event, except for seeing her perhaps once or twice at school parent's evenings, and couldn't remember if she always looked like this, or whether this was because of her time in prison. He certainly didn't feel in any way nervous of working in the house while she was there.

Arthur knew about the effect of loneliness, since the death of his wife, Joan. Their marriage had been happy—well, as happy as any other long-term marriage. Joan had developed cancer some ten years earlier, and bore it stoically. They thought the treatment had been successful, but it sadly returned just over a year later. Within a further year she had succumbed. Since then it had just been him and Dennis. There had been a daughter once. But she had died at just a few months old, many years ago, and they hadn't tried for another baby. It would have been nice to have had a daughter; especially now he was getting along in years. Dennis was a good son, but daughters were special, in his opinion. His best friend Stan had a gem of a daughter, who had done so much for her Dad when he became ill.

Casting these thoughts aside, Arthur was pleased to receive a telephone call from Dorinda, offering him the work.

"Thank you, Miss Lake. I'm pleased to hear that. I don't have a lot of work on at the moment, so I could start next week, if that would suit you?"

"That would be wonderful, Mr Mason. The sooner the better. And please call me Dorinda. Miss Lake reminds me of my days as a teacher, and you are much too old to have been one of my pupils."

She stopped suddenly, perhaps wondering if she had offended Arthur by referring to him as old, but he laughed.

"Thank you, Dorinda. Then you must call me Arthur. I will see you at eight-thirty next Monday then."

"You're working for Miss Lake, the teacher?" Dennis looked a little shocked when his father mentioned his new work over dinner.

"Yes, why not? You expect me to turn her down?"

"You know she went to jail for murder?"

"Yes, and it was manslaughter, actually. There's a difference."

"I know, but…"

"I'm rather hoping you'll come and work with me on this job. It really needs two of us."

His son was silent for a moment, before accepting his Dad's request.

"I guess so. It'll be strange, though, working for one of the teachers."

They began work on the appointed day, and Dennis soon recovered from the shock of being inside the house where a woman was killed. It quickly slipped to the back of his mind, but he couldn't bring himself to call her anything else but Miss. In fact, he had to check himself, when asking her a question, from raising his hand as if they were still in the classroom.

After the first few days, Arthur reflected on how dependable Dennis was becoming, and was glad he had joined him in the business. His skills were improving all the time, and Arthur was patient enough to show him tasks several times before leaving his son to work alone. It gave him a sense of pride to be able to call the business, Arthur Mason and Son, and hoped that, as Dennis became more competent, he would be able to take on more of the work, leaving Arthur to become the backroom boy. He wasn't old enough for retirement just yet, but he had worked solidly since the age of fifteen, and wanted to relax more and discover new pursuits. It had been lonely since his wife had died, and he knew that one day Dennis would leave home. When that day came, he wanted to have built up another life for himself; perhaps a few hobbies; and, who knows, maybe he might even find a good woman to take the place of his dear, departed wife.

CHAPTER 3

ℰLIZABETH COOK

Elizabeth Cook walked along the High Street, a spring in her step, and enjoying the summer sun on her skin, no longer pale, as it had been for so long. It had been two years since transplant surgery had transformed her life, from a dying teenager with cystic fibrosis, into a healthy young woman with a new heart and lungs, and everything to live for.

Many people who hadn't seen her since before the surgery didn't recognise her now. She had been utterly transformed from the pale, wan girl in the wheelchair. Now, her skin glowed, her hair shone, and her face was constantly wreathed in a smile. She felt re-born.

When the call had come, to say that they had a match for her, her father had immediately dropped everything, and they had raced to the hospital with the bag that had been packed, ready, for so long. The hospital wouldn't tell her who the donor was, not even whether it was a woman or a man. Elizabeth wasn't sure she wanted to know, anyway. That was the distressing side of transplants. Someone had to die before another person could live. She tried to put that thought out of her mind.

"What if...? What if...?" But she couldn't ask the question of her father. They both knew what she meant. What if the surgery was unsuccessful? Was this the end of the long and painful road for her? She tried not to think about that too much.

The hospital did all the usual tests to ensure that she was in a fit state to receive the new organs. Her favourite doctor came into her room, his face wreathed in smiles.

"I'm happy to say that all is good, and we will prepare you for surgery immediately."

Elizabeth clenched her father by the hand. For a long time, it had been just the two of them, and she knew that one of the thoughts going through his mind was probably, how can I go on if things go wrong, and I lose my precious daughter? She looked up at him and whispered, "It's all right, Daddy, I'm going to be fine," even though she was whistling in the dark for his sake. But the reality was that, without the transplant, she knew she didn't have long to go, so it was a no-brainer, really. Life, for her, was about to start for the second time.

The surgeon told her later, that within minutes of

receiving the new heart and lungs, they had begun to work strongly, pumping the oxygen and the blood around her body, and he could see the transformation almost straight away. Of course, she would have to take drugs for the rest of her life to stop her body from rejecting the new organs, but that, Elizabeth felt, was a small price to pay.

She had missed so much schooling because of her health, and the school suggested she return and take her final year again. In addition, they suggested she find a private tutor to help her catch up with some of the work she had missed. Someone had suggested Dorinda Lake, a former teacher at the school, who would be able to give her coaching in History, English and Philosophy, the three subjects she had chosen to continue through to Advanced Level exams. She knew Dorinda's history, of course, but, like most other people viewed her as much a victim as a criminal. She felt no compunction about going to meet her.

Miss Lake had responded kindly, and told her how pleased she had been to hear her news about the transplant, and that she would be delighted to give her extra tuition to enable her to catch up what she had missed. Elizabeth obtained a copy of the syllabus, and took it along with her to meet her new tutor at her home.

When she arrived, there were building materials outside the back door, and she heard the sound of workmen in the kitchen. Miss Lake came to greet her, with a warm smile.

"I'm sorry about the workmen. I'm having work done to the kitchen. But if we go into my study, and close the door, I don't think they will be too intrusive."

The study had once been the dining room, and rarely used. Dorinda had painted it a soft lemon, and had new carpet fitted. The dining room table had now become her desk and books lined the shelves on the walls. She had even treated herself to a new laptop. She sat down at the desk, and invited Elizabeth to sit alongside her.

"Let's run through the syllabus first, and try to map out where your strengths and weaknesses are, and where we need to concentrate the work. I can then come up with a timetable to suit you, and we can discuss how many hours per week you will need to see me. I can then set you coursework, which you can prepare at home. Does that sound good for you?"

Elizabeth nodded. "I can't tell you how excited I am, Miss Lake, to be getting this second chance at learning. I missed so much because of my illness."

Dorinda smiled. She hadn't taught Elizabeth at the school, but she remembered seeing her in her wheelchair.

"I'm honoured that you should consider me suitable to help you catch up, Elizabeth. And as I am no longer a school teacher, why don't we relax things a little, and you call me Dorinda?"

After their discussions, it was decided that Elizabeth would visit Dorinda three times weekly, for an hour and a half each time, so that they could work on all three of the subjects, and a modest price was agreed. Now that Dorinda had received the inheritance from her aunt, money wasn't as tight as before, and she genuinely wanted to help the young woman who had been through so much.

As she escorted Elizabeth to the door, Dorinda felt she needed to apologize for the building work going on in the house.

"I'm sorry about the mess and the noise. I hope it won't disturb us too much."

"I'm sure it won't, Miss...Dorinda."

It was going to be hard to get used to this new informality. Walking past the kitchen she spotted the familiar face of Dennis Mason. He had been a year ahead of her at school, but she remembered him, and his pretty girlfriend, Charlotte. The whole school had been devastated when Charlotte was killed. They seemed like a couple who had it all; looks, popularity, love for each other—it just showed, she thought at the time, that everyone had their share of bad luck and tragedy in their lives, sooner or later. At the time, she was only going into school intermittently, because she had become so weak. Her schoolmates looked at her with pity as her motorised wheelchair travelled silently along the corridor. Thoughts of the tragedy had soon been flushed from her mind, however, when the hospital had rung and told her that matching heart and lungs had become available, and her life had been completely transformed.

Dennis glanced up at her as he heard them in the hallway, but there was no sign of recognition from him. And why should there be, she thought. Everyone told her how she had been transformed since the operation. Even looking in the mirror surprised her, when she saw a different face looking back at her. It was as though there were two versions of her; the before and after ones. Inside she was very much the same, but few, if any, knew the inside of her; her mind, her hopes, her dreams. She had hardly dared to dream before the transplant. Her sole concern was surviving long enough to be given the second chance of life. And now she had. It was wonderful, and she was so, so grateful for the family of her donor, for the difficult decision they had faced.

Dennis gave her a quick smile, before turning back to the job in hand. Somehow Elizabeth's heart quickened a little. It seemed a smile of admiration, and she wasn't used to receiving those. She still hadn't transitioned from being the pale, thin invalid to the person she now was.

DENNIS MASON

DENNIS HAD GRIEVED FOR CHARLOTTE, his childhood sweetheart, for a long time; and still did, deep inside. He never spoke of her to anyone, however. His grief and love for her were locked inside him, and talking about her brought it all to the surface again. He knew that life had to go on, as his father was fond of telling him.

"I thought my life was ended when I lost your Mum. But I had to think of you, and that helped me to cope with it."

Dennis didn't remind him that he had lost his Mum, as well as his father losing his wife, so he knew all about grief. But the two sorts of grief were different, he felt. Losing his Mum was like losing his past—his childhood—whereas losing Charlotte was like losing his future—what might have been. But the pain had begun to diminish, as people told him it would. Slowly, he came back to the world of his youth, and knew that Charlotte wouldn't have wanted him to spend his life grieving for her.

Joining his father in the business, and learning a trade, helped in the process of moving on. The future became less bleak. He enjoyed working with his Dad. They didn't talk very much while they worked—Arthur preferred to concentrate on the job in hand.

"When you're working with sharp tools, and expensive materials, you need to keep your wits about you," was his mantra, and Dennis came to agree. He gained great satisfaction with seeing two well-cut pieces of timber fit together perfectly, due to the skills he was gaining.

But during the twice daily tea breaks—Arthur wouldn't allow for more—they chatted about all sorts of issues, and Dennis felt he was gaining a greater understanding of his father. He noticed, too, how his father's face lit up when Miss Lake came into the room to check on progress. He seemed, to Dennis's inexpert eye, to have developed a bit of a crush on her. It wasn't as though the former teacher was particularly attractive. As far as Dennis was concerned, she was quite ordinary. But, just as in the classroom her face had lit up when teaching her beloved history, so it began to light up when chatting to Arthur. Dennis didn't tease his father about it, however. Losing the love of his life had instilled in him a compassion that probably wasn't present before. He was a kinder person because of it. He decided not to mention his observations to his father, but would wait and see how things developed.

Miss Lake was, it appeared, taking on some private tuition. Well that made sense, he thought. She wasn't yet at retirement age, and she couldn't go back to teaching after being in jail for killing her mother, so she had to earn money somehow. Although, he conjectured, with the work being done to the house, she clearly wasn't broke.

He spotted the pretty young woman coming up the path

to the back door, and wondered about her. She was local, and had been to the same school as him, but he couldn't recall seeing her there. She always had a smile on her face. He noticed that, because so many of the girls her age seemed to walk around looking miserable, as though they had lost a fortune. What was wrong with looking cheerful, he wondered, and guessed it wasn't 'cool' to be happy?

She lifted her head, and saw Dennis watching her. Raising her hand in greeting, she gave him a grin, before vanishing out of sight as she stepped into the house. He could hear her greeting Miss Lake before they disappeared into the room where they worked. Seeing her grin made him strangely happy for the first time in many months, and he hoped he might get to speak to her before too long.

The opportunity came two days later, when, as he and his father started their afternoon tea break, Miss Lake came in and began chatting to Arthur. Dennis decided to wander out into the garden and enjoy the afternoon sun, and give his Dad a bit of space. His reward came when, a couple of minutes later, the young woman arrived for her lesson.

"Hello. It's a lovely afternoon, isn't it?"

Her voice was soft and gentle, and her smile was radiant. He thought he had never seen a prettier girl.

"Yes, it is. You've come for your lesson?"

That was a silly question, he realised, just a second after the words had left his mouth. Of course she was here for her lesson. But she showed no amusement or scorn at his observation.

"Yes, I'm here for history today."

"That's good. Miss Lake is a really great teacher. She took

me for history at school. She's so enthusiastic about it, you can't help enjoying it."

"I never had her as a teacher at Westlands High, but everyone said how good she was."

"I didn't realise you went there too. I don't remember you."

"I was a year below you at school. People don't tend to notice those younger than themselves, do they?"

She paused for a moment, as if uncertain whether to proceed; but eventually said her piece.

"I remember seeing you and Charlotte Trent together. I was so very sorry to hear what had happened."

Her face had clouded over and there was genuine sadness there.

"Thank you. It was...it was hard when it happened. I'm starting to get used to it now, but sometimes, when I wake up in the morning, I forget she's gone, and think of something I want to tell her."

"I hope I haven't made you sad by talking about her?"

"No...no, it's fine. I hate it when people avoid talking about her; as though she was never here."

Elizabeth gave a half smile.

"Well, I'd better not keep the teacher waiting."

Dennis watched as she walked into the house.

"Nice girl," he thought.

NOW THE ICE had been broken, he looked out for her on the days she was due for a lesson, and somehow contrived to be in the hallway, or on the garden path, as Elizabeth arrived. They exchanged a few words every time. One day, Dennis plucked up the courage to ask her something that had been in his mind for a week or so.

"Would you like to meet me for a coffee on Saturday at that new coffee shop in town? We could perhaps walk along the river path if the weather is good."

Elizabeth paused for a moment, running the question through her mind, no doubt.

"Yes. That would be nice. I'd be free about three o'clock, if that's alright with you?"

The date was set, and Dennis walked back into the kitchen with a big grin on his face. His father had seen the meeting of the two through the window, and couldn't help teasing his son gently.

"You two seem to be getting on very well these days. Anything to share?"

Dennis just grinned, but said nothing. He wasn't yet ready to discuss Elizabeth with his father. Besides, he could talk. Every time Denis turned around, his Dad and Miss Lake were deep in conversation, and his father looked at his former teacher a lot more than he looked at most of his clients.

Saturday afternoon was, thankfully, dry and sunny. He turned up at the coffee shop in his best jeans, and a new shirt he'd bought the previous week—the first new clothes for a long time. Elizabeth was already there, sitting at a table in the window, wearing a pretty blue and white cotton summer dress. Her long hair was hanging loose on her shoulders, and Dennis thought she looked even prettier than normal.

"Hi, I hope I haven't kept you waiting?"

"No, I'm always early for things."

"Well that's better than keeping people waiting every time."

He remembered that this had been one of Charlotte's few failing. How many times had he stood outside the cinema, or the dance hall, waiting for her?

"Coffee?"

"Mmm, cappuccino please."

Dennis ordered two cappuccinos.

"I can't believe I never noticed you at school. I know you were younger, but I'm sure I would have heard from my friends about a pretty girl like you."

Elizabeth wasn't sure whether to tell him that people rarely noticed the pale, thin girl in a wheelchair, as she had been then. She decided not to reveal her past just yet. Her illness and the times when she felt that death was close, had been a grim time. But her new life, since the transplant, was a joyful one, and she preferred not to think back to the grim times of her childhood.

"Oh, I don't think I was all that pretty in the school uniform. It was so drab. Plus, I was very shy."

Dennis didn't pursue the matter, and they chatted about inconsequential things like favourite bands, television programmes and suchlike.

Walking along the river path, a favourite place for young courting couples, getting to know each other, in the late afternoon sun, was a delight, Dennis thought. It had been a long time since he had felt happy and content to be in someone's company. It almost felt as though he had known this girl forever. There were no awkward silences. No stumbling over words. He wanted to take hold of her hand, but felt it was perhaps a little too early in their friendship for physical contact. His father had brought him up to be respectful towards girls, and was almost old-fashioned in his courteous behaviour.

ARTHUR MASON

ARTHUR SMILED to see the developing friendship between his son and the young pupil of Dorinda Lake. It was good to see Dennis noticing pretty girls again. He had mourned Charlotte for a long time, but Arthur felt it was time for him to re-join the world of the living. He, too, had struggled emotionally after his wife died, but it had been a long time since that happened. Once or twice he had contemplated whether to begin a relationship, but the women he had met somehow didn't measure up to his dear, departed wife.

Meeting Dorinda Lake had triggered his latent interest in the opposite sex. She was fairly ordinary to look at—but then, so was he—but she possessed a charming manner and a bright intelligence, with an interest in so many different subjects. He could stand and talk to her for hours, until he remembered that he was supposed to be at her home working. Dorinda seemed happy to chat to him too. She never mentioned the business of her mother, and her time in jail, and Arthur carefully avoided the subject.

When the two men stopped for their afternoon tea-break, Dorinda would often appear with a packet of chocolate biscuits, and Dennis, wanting to give his father a little space, would go out into the garden with his mug of tea, often to await the arrival of Elizabeth.

"He's a nice young man, your son."

Dorinda had always liked him when he was at school, and was pleased he had retained his pleasant manner.

"Yes, he's a good lad. I'm glad to be his Dad. He's had a tough time; losing his Mum and then his girlfriend. Some lads would have gone off the rails; but not him. It looks like he's quite taken with your young pupil."

"Yes, I've noticed them chatting a few times. I expect they know each other from school. Nice girl."

She thought about mentioning Elizabeth's medical history, but decided it would be indiscreet. A lot of people probably knew she had had a transplant; maybe Arthur did too. But it wasn't a good idea to discuss her pupils with other people.

Arthur knew that Dennis had already been on a date with Elizabeth, but didn't say anything to Dorinda. He knew his son wouldn't like having his affairs discussed with his former teacher. He was actually toying with the idea of taking a leaf from his son's book and inviting Dorinda to have dinner with him one night. Perhaps he should wait until the job was finished, just in case it didn't work out. It probably wasn't a good idea to mix business with pleasure. He'd be done here in a week or so; he'd wait until then before chancing his arm.

He changed the subject to the paint colour of the wall above the tiled area in the new kitchen.

"Did you decide on the colour yet? I reckon I will need to get it soon. I can call and pick it up on the way here tomorrow morning."

They both looked again at the paint chart Arthur had brought from the store. Huddled together, looking at the colours, was the closest he had yet been to Dorinda, and he smelt a faint perfume from her skin; maybe the soap she used. These sorts of things he missed from not having a woman in his life. He remembered how his wife used to like a particular luxury soap for her birthday, whereas now, he and Dennis made do with the cheapest soap, bought when they went food shopping.

CHAPTER 4

*G*RANT LE FEVRE – *Yemen, some years earlier*

THE SUN BEAT down mercilessly on to the sand and rocks of the desert of southern Yemen, causing a heat haze to distort the view. There was little shade in the middle of this heated oven of a place – just a few boulders, beneath one of which the man was lying in an effort to escape the direct sunshine. He tried to sleep, but it eluded him – it was just too hot. Opening the water carrier lying at his side, he took a sip – rationing this precious commodity that would make the difference between life and death in this godforsaken place. He removed his headdress to enable his head to cool and loosened his footah, the traditional Yemeni skirt that was wrapped around his lower body and kept up by a belt. He daren't remove his sandals however, in case he had to move off in a hurry.

Close by, a snake hissed as it went after a small lizard, and the man froze in case the snake turned towards him. He was afraid of very little in life, but snakes made him nervous.

Gradually the sun began to set and the man knew that he would soon be able to move off under cover of darkness. He shook his water container and decided that it would probably only last him for another twenty-four hours. After that, unless he could refill it, or find some way of making contact with the Boss and get himself extracted from this hellhole, then he was in big trouble.

He tried not to think about the events of the last two days. There would be time for reflection and analysis in the weeks or months ahead. Regrets and grief about his lost comrades would come eventually, but for now he must concentrate on survival.

As the darkness descended, the man wound his headdress around his filthy and uncombed hair and tightened the belt around his footah. Getting his bearings from where the sun had set and the position of the emerging stars he began to walk. Every muscle in his body ached almost beyond endurance and he was weak from lack of food and water, but he thought that he might be getting closer to the coast. He concentrated on simply putting one foot in front of the other and pushed all other thoughts to the edge of his mind.

He had been walking for around five hours when a sound made him freeze. It wasn't a human noise, but more that of an animal. He peered anxiously ahead into the dark and could just make out the outline of some trees. Could it be a waterhole? If so, it might be the miracle that would save his life. He crept forward silently and saw the outline of a pair of camels about twenty feet away. Where there were camels there would almost certainly be people. He wondered if he should risk filling his water carrier and perhaps steal some food, or whether to give the place a wide berth and continue walking. Hunger and thirst overcame the fear of discovery and he crept closer until he spotted the small waterhole in front of him. About five metres to his right he could see the shapes of two people, wrapped in blankets. The faint glow of a campfire was visible and the smell of cooked meat lingered in the air, tantalizing the man's aching and empty stomach.

He crawled slowly towards the waterhole, a few inches at a time and gently dipped his water container into the small, dark pool. He couldn't resist dipping his hand into the water and bringing the damp fingers up to his cracked and sore lips. One of the camels made a faint noise and moved its body into a more comfortable sitting position. He froze, wondering if the sound would wake the sleeping men, and waited a minute or so before he was sure that there was no movement from the camels' owners, before edging backwards at a glacial pace with the water carrier and laying it gently under a palm tree. Was it worth going back for some of the food that may remain in the cooking pot? He had not eaten for two days and did not know how much further he could walk on an empty stomach, and the pain in his gut was beginning to torment him. He decided that he would have to take the risk, if he was to find the strength to continue walking. The only weapon he had managed to hang on to had been his knife, which he held in his right hand as he crept forward towards the cooking pot, still hanging over the fire, every fibre of his senses on the alert for danger. There was no movement from the heaped blankets. He extended his left hand towards the cooking pot, but before he could reach it, he was jumped. A heavy body fell on top of him and what felt like a knife came across his throat. He rolled instinctively away from the knife, but rolled into the dying fire. So did his attacker.

"Fuck I'm in the fire."

The voice was American. Thank God. He found his voice and shouted out the call sign and name of the operation so he could be identified before another knife could reach his throat.

"Cougar six zero. Cougar six zero. American. American."

"It's Mac. Where the fuck have you been? We've been searching for you for days. Where are the others? Are they with you?"

A hand shot out and pulled him to his feet, whilst the man who had fallen into the fire was frantically beating out the glowing embers that had attached themselves to his clothes. Despite the adrenaline that was still pumping around his body, the man they called Mac suddenly felt drained of energy and realized that he had had a lucky escape. If these guys had been a fraction of a second quicker, he would probably be dead by now. His hunger and exhaustion had nearly cost him his life. He recognized the voices of Buzz and Ray, two men from his unit, and in a quiet voice he answered their query.

"No there's only me. The other two didn't make it."

All three men were quiet for a few moments – digesting the news that two of their number would not be going home.

· · ·

PRESENT TIME

GRANT AWOKE WITH A START. It had been the dream again; the one featuring his lucky escape many years earlier, when he had been part of an American Special Forces unit, conducting clandestine reconnaissance in Yemen—a godforsaken, impoverished country, few back then had even heard of. He had been known as Mac at that time, and not by his real name of Grant Le Fevre. His surname was courtesy of his father, a French national, whom his American mother had married shortly before Grant's birth. Unfortunately, the marriage hadn't lasted, and Grant's mother took her son back to the US, to bring him up as an American. He often wondered what had happened to his father, who lost touch with them quite quickly after the divorce. His mother told him he had been in the French Foreign Legion, and Grant sometimes wondered if that was the reason behind his desire to join the armed forces. He had served eight years in the army, before applying to transfer to special forces. Yes, it had sometimes been exciting, often dangerous, but after his time in Yemen, he had decided that the life was no longer for him.

Returning to civilian life, in his mid-thirties, he swapped his gun for a camera, and continued to roam the world as a freelance war photographer, supplying iconic pictures to some of the world's media, and winning two awards on the way. As he lay in a foxhole in Afghanistan, alongside a unit of British Royal Marines, he wondered what he was doing, still putting his life on the line, and trying to interest a largely disinterested world in what was happening beyond their shores.

As he listened to the British accents around him, he thought back to a woman he had met while briefly living in London; Jennifer Blake, a journalist with The Times. Like him, she travelled the world, and it was hard to make a relationship work under those circumstances. He had been very struck with her, he remembered. He loved her British sense of humour and her intelligence—not a bad-looker either, he recalled. She had joked with him.

"One day, when we've both got the travel bug out of our system, and we end up in the same country, we must carry on this conversation."

That was said in a Paris hotel room, where they had stayed for a dirty weekend. Neither of them was in a committed relationship; he separated, she never married; and he wondered if she had meant it. Perhaps, when he returned from this trip, he would look her up. It had been several years since they had last met, and neither had been good at keeping in touch. He hoped nothing bad had happened to her. He was sure he would have heard on the grapevine if it had.

As LUCK WOULD HAVE IT, his next job involved a trip to London, where several Middle Eastern leaders were assembled for a meeting, involving the troubles in Syria. Grant's brief was to photograph some of the leaders involved, and plan for a trip to Syria to follow, so he could see the chaos on the ground for himself. He was working with a journalist from The New York Times, whom he had known for a long time. Perhaps he might get to London with a few days to spare, and look up Jennifer Blake, and see how she was.

He knew his days spent photographing in war zones were coming to an end. There was only so far he could stretch his luck, and he was getting too old to share foxholes with young soldiers. Perhaps he should consider retirement? Perhaps write that autobiography he had been thinking about for a while? He had some interesting stories to tell, provided anyone wanted to read them.

So it was that a month later found him stepping on to the Tarmac at Heathrow Airport, three days prior to his first scheduled meeting with Carl, his journalist colleague. He had sent an email to Jennifer's last-known address, and was pleasantly surprised when she replied to it with enthusiasm.

Hey Grant,

Great to hear from you. I've often wondered where you were and what you are up to. After my health issues, I had to take early retirement from the paper, but I'm doing well and have actually started writing a novel.

Like you, there's no one in my life right now, and it would be great to meet up with you in London, and talk about old times. Call me when you arrive and we can arrange when and where to meet.

Jennifer x

As soon as he reached his hotel in Central London, he gave her a call on the number she had sent. She answered on the third ring.

"Grant, how are you? Great to hear your voice again."

"You too, Jennifer. How long's it been? Three years? Four years?"

"Must be four at least. I've been retired over three years."

"I would love to meet you for dinner, if you're able to make it up to London. I have three free days, before I have to work for a further three. Then it's off to Syria for the usual junket."

Jennifer laughed.

"I understand only too well. Thankfully, my suitcases are safely stowed in the loft, although I sometimes think wistfully of long-ago trips. Do you remember that trip we took to Siem Reap – must have been at least twenty-five years ago – when we found the hotel fully booked? That was fun, wasn't it?"

Grant smiled at the memories. It had been a little side trip; one of several they had made over the years. They had both been covering the elections in Phnom Penh, Cambodia, when Jennifer had persuaded him to see the beautiful Angkor Wat Temple. But Cambodia hadn't yet got back into the full tourism mode. Three plane loads of visitors arrived from the capital, but only the lucky ones in the first two managed to gain a hotel room. The local tourist office had persuaded some locals to vacate their home for the night to enable the foreigners to stay. It had all added to the fun of the trip, though, for the two of them. Certainly, Grant, being ex-army, had slept in far worse places.

"It certainly was. And being there with you made it a night to remember."

She laughed. "You old smoothie."

"Well I try. How about we meet tomorrow night at my

hotel and go someplace for dinner? There's absolutely no obligation on you to stay the night with me, but you know the invitation is always there. It's entirely up to you."

"Sounds good to me. I'll be there at seven, if that's okay with you."

She hadn't committed herself to whether she would stay over. Probably doesn't want to be taken for granted, he thought.

THE NEXT EVENING, still feeling a little jetlagged, Grant sat in the hotel lobby and saw the familiar face appear in the entrance. He noticed she was carrying a small overnight bag, and smiled inwardly, hoping that was a good sign for the night ahead. He walked over to greet her, and kissed her on the cheek.

"Jennifer, I swear you look younger and more lovely every time we meet. I simply refuse to believe that you are retired."

"I took early retirement, don't forget," she replied with a wink.

"The restaurant is just a few doors down. How about we take your bag up to my room, and you can freshen up if you want. Then we can have a drink in the hotel bar before dinner."

Fifteen minutes later they were down in the hotel bar. The waiter came to serve them.

"What would you like, Jennifer? A glass of champagne, perhaps? Or a cocktail?"

"Champagne sounds good."

Grant ordered the same for them both.

"You look as great as always. What's your secret?"

"Thank you. Living the life I love, thankfully. You look well yourself. What have you been up to lately?"

They filled each other in on events of the past few years. Grant was already aware she had had breast cancer some years earlier and hoped fervently there hadn't been a recurrence of that, to cause her early retirement.

"I hope you had no more cancer scares."

"No, I was lucky. It was caught early, and I think it's gone for good. But it made me reassess my priorities. Travelling for the paper had become stressful. I had managed to put away some savings, plus my parents had left me a house and some money. So, I made the decision to give up the city smoke, and retire to my home town. I now write fiction. Not very successfully, I might add."

"Glad to hear you had no more cancer trouble. I think you were wise to make the move. Constant stress and travelling isn't good for any of us as we age. I'm thinking of giving up the war photography, and finding a quiet spot to settle down, and maybe grow vegetables."

Jennifer smiled.

"I've never thought of you as a gardener, somehow. It seems too tranquil a hobby for you. But maybe that's what you need right now."

"Maybe I've lain in one too many foxholes and been shot at too many times. The novelty has worn off. Time for a different life."

They finished the champagne, and walked the fifty yards along the street to a small, Thai restaurant.

"This okay for you, I hope?" He had considered it a safe bet, as they had dined together in Thailand once.

"Yes, lovely. I haven't eaten Thai food for a long while."

"I remember it well—a great break in Phuket. We had a lot of fun there, I recall."

He winked at Jennifer and she grinned back; a shiver of expectation passing through Grant, at the time spent together in Thailand, and the possibility of a repeat performance that night.

The evening passed off very well. They still felt relaxed in each other's company, despite the length of time since they had seen each other. They laughed at each other's jokes, and recalled more memories from places they had been together. Grant couldn't for the life of him understand why he had let this woman slip through his fingers. Maybe this time…

As they walked back to the hotel, Jennifer linked her arm in his. They had both had a couple of glasses of wine with dinner—just enough to feel relaxed and mellow, without being at risk of saying foolish things. As they reached the lobby of the hotel, Grant took one of her hands in his.

"I'm not taking anything for granted. The decision about whether to stay the night or not is entirely yours, and I won't be annoyed if you decide to return home tonight."

"Grant, I can think of nothing nicer than staying overnight with you."

AND SO IT BEGAN AGAIN. Their on/off relationship was back on once more. As he caressed Jennifer's body, in his bed that night, Grant made a vow that this time he wouldn't allow them to drift apart again. They fit together so well—not just physically, but mentally and emotionally, in every way. It was time he took off his wandering boots, and enjoyed the benefits of a stable home for once.

As she sat up in bed the following morning, sipping the coffee that Grant had just made, Jennifer appeared to be having similar thoughts.

"It's sad that you're here for such a short visit. When are we going to spend more time together? You know you're always welcome to come and stay with me any time."

"That, my dear, is a tantalising thought. It's about time I left the globetrotting to my younger colleagues. I'm back in London in about a month, for a week or so. Why don't we both give some thought to getting together on a more permanent basis?"

"That sounds, to me, a wonderful idea."

As they kissed goodbye, and Jennifer took the train back home, she mused on whether her life would turn another corner.

CHAPTER 5

*J*ENNIFER BLAKE

GROWING up as an only child in Swinbury hadn't been easy for Jennifer Blake. She had once had a twin sister, who died at the age of four. Although he had never said as such, she had always felt that her father blamed her for the accident that befell her sister, who was younger than her by twenty-five minutes. They had been told not to leave the garden, and especially not to go close to the river that was just twenty yards from the back of the house. The gate was always latched and kept closed, but the refuse collector had left it open that day. Jennifer, being the bolder and more adventurous of the two girls, decided to go through it, and urged her sister to follow.

As they walked along the riverbank, picking wildflowers, Juliet had slipped on a patch of mud, and within seconds had plunged into the river. Neither girl could swim, and all the four-year-old Jennifer could think of to do was to run home and alert her mother. It had been six hours before they found Juliet's body, tangled in the weeds. Their father hardly spoke for days; so traumatised was he over what had happened. Even when he began to speak again, he never discussed the accident with Jennifer. But she grew up with the feeling that she was to blame for her sister's death. If only she had listened to her father's exhortations to stay in the garden.

The years passed, and Jennifer longed to leave home as soon as she was able – away from her miserable father and unemotional mother. She recognised, however, that if she wanted to get anywhere in life, she needed good A levels results, that would get her into university. She worked hard and achieved the results she wanted, and was accepted for an English degree at Cambridge; beyond her wildest dreams. She confided to her English teacher that her ambition was to be a journalist, and travel the world.

"I think you will make an excellent journalist, Jennifer. Work hard and make us proud."

It touched Jennifer that the praise she received from her teacher was praise that she had always longed to hear from her parents. It had been sadly lacking throughout her child-hood, and she was convinced it was entirely due to her twin sister's death.

Cambridge gave her the freedom she had longed for, and she adored the life of a student. There were a few boyfriends, but no one special. She didn't want to be tied down in a rela-tionship at this point in her life. She graduated with a First-

Class Honours degree in English, and felt the sky was now her limit. When she told her parents, they were, of course, pleased for her, but as usual, there was little jubilation from them. In her disappointment and pain, she lashed out, in a way she never had before.

"I realise, of course, that if Juliet had lived, she would have probably achieved far more than me. I can never compensate for causing her death, no matter how hard I try."

Her father froze, and looked at her with shock and amazement.

"You didn't cause her death. What made you think that? It wasn't your fault she died."

There was silence for a moment as all the pain and the hurt of sixteen years came flooding to the surface. Jennifer's voice rose to a crescendo; to a level she had never used before.

"You've always blamed me. I know that. You can't deny it now. I've lived with this guilt all these years. Nothing I do can ever bring her back."

By now, tears were streaming down her face, and she grabbed the back of the kitchen chair to steady herself. But her eyes were on her father's face. It seemed frozen in shock. His mouth moved, but nothing came out. He sank down on a chair and put his face in his hands, great gulping sobs coming from him as though a valve had been opened, allowing years of pent-up grief to come to the surface.

Jennifer's mother simply stood with her mouth open, staring at her husband, as though she couldn't recognise him. Her face became more animated than it had been for years, as she looked with sorrow at her daughter. She spoke quietly and relatively unemotionally.

"He doesn't blame you for Juliet's death. He has always blamed me. I was the one who was supposed to look after you—to care for you both—and your father thinks I let you both down."

Graham Blake's sobs slowed, and then stopped. He looked up at both his wife and daughter.

"Neither of you were to blame for Juliet's death. No one was. It was an accident; a terrible, terrible accident." He paused for a moment, as if to collect his thoughts. He looked agonisingly at his daughter. "I'm so sorry you felt all this time that you were to blame, Jennifer. I'm so sorry…"

Turning to his wife, he repeated his plea for forgiveness.

"I shouldn't have blamed you, Jean. It was wrong of me. I was just lashing out in my pain." His voice faded away as his wife moved towards him. She put her hand on his shoulder, and for a moment it seemed as though her husband was going to turn and fall into her arms, but he didn't. He just looked overwhelmed. There had been so much grief; so much pain over such a long time; it would take a long time to process what had just happened. They merely stood and looked at one another. But Jennifer had no such inhibitions. She reached out and took her father's hand tightly, as tears ran down her cheeks.

"I thought…I thought…"

The tears became heart wrenching sobs as the pain of so many years came to the surface, and her father couldn't ignore the pain on his daughter's face. He pulled her into his body and hugged her tight, while choking back his own tears.

"I'm sorry, I'm sorry," was all he could say.

Jennifer's mother came into the huddle, putting her arms

around the shoulders of her remaining daughter, trying to comfort her.

"Shhh! Don't cry, my dear. It wasn't your fault. Nothing was your fault. You were just a child."

Jennifer felt a weight removed from her back as she released the burden of guilt about her twin sister's death. At the same time, however, she felt intense sadness for the wasted years between her and her parents, when each of them had been cocooned inside their own private hell following the drowning. It had almost destroyed her family, but maybe, just maybe, they could salvage something from what had happened, and reconstruct something of the family who remained.

FROM THAT DAY ONWARDS, it was as though the family had come to a new understanding. It wasn't easy to suddenly begin communicating after so many years of silence, but Jennifer developed a new understanding of her parents. They may never regain the closeness they had once enjoyed as a family of four, but much of the pain had now faded.

Jennifer began her career as a journalist with one of the smaller daily papers, but her eyes were set on one of the bigger, better known ones, and within five years gained a position with The Times.

"What are your ultimate ambitions?" said the interviewer, all those years ago.

"To be a foreign correspondent," she replied, without hesitation. She witnessed the occasional entry into the newsroom of one of the titans of the newspaper's foreign correspondents, returning from a war zone, or a big political jamboree overseas, and saw how revered and respected most of them were. She noted that most were men, but there were a few women among their number.

Slowly she climbed the career ladder, until, at last, at the age of thirty, she was admitted to the hallowed halls of the foreign correspondents. Her jobs were quite small and unimportant at first, but she impressed her bosses with her dogged determination to get the story and her willingness to worm her way into the confidence of world leaders and get them to open up to her.

She had been in her early thirties when she and Grant first met. He had been a freelance photographer who had occasionally supplied pictures for The Times, and knowing his background as a special forces soldier with the US army, had chatted to him in a bar in Phnom Penh, the capital of Cambodia, one night, trying to get some background infor- mation on one of the former Khmer Rouge leaders, now standing for election at the first elections following the liber- ation of that country by the Vietnamese army. All three of them were staying in the huge, modern hotel, the Cambodi- ana, and Jennifer had an appointment booked with the Cambodian politician the following day.

Jennifer and Grant had dinner together in the hotel, while Grant gave her the benefit of his knowledge about the man she was to interview.

"Can I trust what he says?" she asked him.

"Ha, ha, no more than any other politician," was the response from a man who found it hard to place any trust in politicians.

They talked about each other's backgrounds and experi- ences so far, and Jennifer felt drawn to this man who had lived on the edge of danger for so long. He talked slowly and quietly, as though used to measuring his words, and as the evening wore on, she knew she wanted to hear those slow-measured words whispered into her ear, as they made love.

That night, they did what thousands of people who find themselves a long way from home do, they clung together in mutual enjoyment of each other's bodies, and home didn't seem so far away.

So, the pattern was set. No promises were made; just an understanding that, when time and circumstances permitted, they would meet and resume their casual affair. Sometimes there would be months between meetings, and occasionally they were lucky and bumped into each other on a more frequent basis. Private jokes were developed. Messages were sent to each other's email accounts. Jennifer learned how Grant enjoyed his coffee in the morning, and he learned that, being British, she would never start the day without a cup of tea. The future was never discussed, but there was an under-lying assumption that one day their relationship might become more permanent, so long as neither of them met anyone else in the meantime.

One day, Jennifer told Grant about Juliet; the first person to have ever heard her story. He didn't try to issue dumb platitudes, but simply held her close and kissed her forehead when the story was complete. She didn't know why she had told him the story of her long-dead sister, when she hadn't revealed it to even her best friends, but she felt a strange sense of calm after she had finished. She didn't mention the rift that had taken place between her mother, father and herself over so many years, however. Perhaps, one day...

Travelling back home, after the reunion with Grant in

London, she thought hard about what he had suggested. Could they turn what had been a casual fling, over many years, into something more permanent? Could she bear to share her home, the home that had once been her parents when they lived, with him?

Her parents had died within a year of each other. First her father developed heart trouble, and was found dead in his armchair by her mother one evening. His heart had simply stopped beating. Jennifer's mother stayed in the house until breast cancer claimed her, just a year after her husband's death. Jennifer was devastated. She had long since forgiven them for the trauma of growing up thinking she was to blame for Juliet's death, and they had managed to develop a close bond in the intervening years. Now, following the death of her mother, she was alone in the world. The house and its contents were all left to her, and she considered selling it and buying one elsewhere for her retirement, but in the end her own illness made her reconsider.

Her doctor suggested that, because of the breast cancer that had claimed her mother, Jennifer should be checked for the condition herself. It came as a devastating shock to find that she, too, had the disease. She was numb. Did this mean that she would die too? But it turned out that hers was caught at a very early stage, and her mother's had been in its very late stage by the time it was discovered. She had the option of simply having the lump removed, or the more drastic course of a double mastectomy and breast reconstruction. It was a tough decision to make, but in the end, she opted for caution and had both breasts removed. The reconstruction was carried out by a top-class surgeon, paid for from the private medical insurance provided by the paper, and once the scars beneath each breast had healed and faded, there was little to show there had ever been a problem.

She had cancelled a planned weekend with Grant, and turned down his offer to fly over from Paris to see her when she told him what had happened.

"I'll be fine. You would only be able to stay for a couple of days, and would see me at my worst. I would rather get it all over and done with, and then we can meet up again as soon as circumstances permit."

When they met again, four months later, and spent the night in a hotel in Cairo, where a meeting of Arab heads of states was taking place, Grant made a point of kissing and fondling her new breasts in the same way as he had the old ones.

"I was tempted to ask for a slightly larger size; I've always thought mine were a little too small—but in the end I opted to keep the size I was familiar with."

"Your breasts are the perfect size and shape. I'm glad you didn't change them."

He bent his head and kissed them gently, and Jennifer was relieved that they had crossed the hurdle without any awkwardness or shyness from either of them.

THE DAY ARRIVED when Grant was due to fly in—initially to stay for a month, but with the likelihood that if everything worked out well, they would remain together for good. In the years since her parents had died, Jennifer had changed a lot in the house, having a new kitchen and bathroom, and re-decorating throughout. She had also replaced much of her parents old fashioned furniture with pieces she had bought from her life in London, or from her travels abroad. She hoped that her American friend liked it. In the years that they had known one another, their meetings had taken place almost entirely abroad in hotels. He had stayed a couple of times at her London rented flat, but she had never visited him at his home in the US. There was a lot to discover, she mused. Was she mad in making this decision at this point in her life? Well, time would tell, she thought, with slight trepidation.

She drove to the station in time to meet the London train as it arrived. There was Grant's cheerful face as, laden with bags and suitcases, he climbed down on to the platform.

"Have you any idea how much it cost me in excess baggage to bring this lot on the plane?"

"Well you are moving home, aren't you? It's not like going on a two-week vacation."

She helped him pile the bags into the car and they eventually turned to greet each other. He wrapped his arms around her, and she welcomed him into her life; still a little nervous about whether they had both made the right decision.

IT WAS NEARLY midnight as they lay in bed—pleasantly tired after sorting out Grant's closet space, eating a dinner they cooked together, and making love in a sweet and gentle way.

"Why do you think we didn't get together before? Why did we waste so much time?"

Grant propped himself up on one arm, and looked down

at her face—a familiar face; still beautiful, despite the passing of the years.

"I've asked myself that several times. I suppose we were never in the same country long enough at the same time. It would have been very difficult to maintain a stable relationship. Do you regret waiting so long?"

"Sometimes I wish we had been together more often. But I'm happy that it has developed into something more permanent; assuming, of course, that more permanent is something we both want. It's very different being with someone 24/7, than the excitement of snatched weekends and trysts in exotic foreign locations. Do you think we can stand the mundaneness of food shopping on a Friday afternoon in town, or settling down to watch an old movie with a bottle of wine?"

Grant smiled, and lay back down on the bed, resting his arm casually over Jennifer's no longer quite so flat stomach.

"I can think of nothing nicer than watching an old movie, and drinking a glass of wine with you—having bought it together at the supermarket."

She sighed with contentment. If her decision to admit Grant into her home and life like this would be considered by some to be crazy; it was, she thought, something she couldn't regret.

CHAPTER 6

GRACE BENNETT

GRACE HAD BEEN a teenager when she saw the first women being ordained as Church of England vicars. She had been going through a religious phase at the time, and seeing these pioneer women in the church inspired her. There and then she decided she would become a vicar when she was old enough.

Her parents, while not overly dismayed, were surprised, and perhaps a little disappointed. Grace was a clever girl, and was expected to go to university and have a stellar career in perhaps the Law, her father thought. She was a pretty girl, and popular with the boys at her school Her parents didn't know where her calling had arisen, but had no objection to their daughter's choice of career.

At school she had been a star pupil and was universally popular. Several of the boys regretted that religion had become the heart of her life – although becoming a vicar didn't preclude her from becoming a wife and mother. Nevertheless, she had decided that the church would take priority, and marriage would be a long way into the future, if at all.

In 1998, aged eighteen, Grace's calling into the church was as strong as ever, and she began four years at Theological college, which she enjoyed enormously; leaving as one of their most promising students—maybe even becoming a candidate as a Bishop, should women eventually be accepted into the higher echelons of the church.

Her first post had been as a curate in a church in Liverpool; a demanding job in an area of poverty and high crime rates. Nevertheless, she threw herself into the work with enthusiasm—until that night.

Leaving the church late one evening, after preparing for a christening the following day, she was accosted by a man; someone she later found out had mental health problems.

"Hello, lady vicar. You're here late."

"Oh, you startled me. Yes, I've been preparing for tomorrow."

She tried to walk around the man, who smelled of alcohol and was badly dressed. Perhaps he was a vagrant. The church was often seen as a sanctuary for down and outs. She smiled, and tried to look confident, but fear had already gripped her stomach.

Attempting to step around him, he was alert enough to

prevent it, and grabbed her by the arm, pushing her back into the church, through the door she hadn't yet locked. She felt sick, realising what may lie ahead. Everything happened so quickly. The man's demeanour turned nasty as he began to hit her. Trying to escape from him, she tripped and landed hard on the stone flagstones. The fall switched her from the paralysis of terror into survival mode, and began to fight back, which seemed to surprise her assailant. Catching him unawares, she lashed out with the sturdy boots she was wearing under her cassock, and landed a powerful kick in his groin. He was winded, and in pain. Before he had the chance to retaliate, she was on her feet and raced through the door, through the graveyard and on to the street.

She searched desperately for someone who might help her; fearful that the man would recover and soon be after her. As luck would have it, a couple of men were returning home after a late-night shift in the docks, and became her saviours. One rang for the police, while another stood guard in case Grace's attacker appeared.

THE MAN WAS CAUGHT a few hours later, and eventually sectioned under the Mental Health Act; not being of sufficiently sound mind to stand trial. Meanwhile, Grace, in the company of the vicar's wife, lived the episode over and over in her mind—unable to free her mind from the very real terror of what had happened.

"I'm very relieved he is locked up, my dear."

The Bishop was sitting in the cosy sitting room of the vicarage, together with Grace's immediate boss, the vicar, several days later. All three were drinking tea. "Are you feeling more relieved, now you know he's no longer around?"

At that precise moment, Grace didn't feel she would ever feel relieved or calm about anything, ever again. Her inner peace had been shattered, and her mind was torn about the way ahead. Right now, her instinct was to get as far away from Liverpool as was possible. She wasn't even sure she wanted to remain in the Church. The Vicar, a kindly man in his fifties, seemed to understand this. He had a daughter of a similar age, and the attack on Grace had hit him hard when he thought about it happening to his own child.

He reached out and touched the back of Grace's hand lightly.

"Why don't you go to stay with your family for a few weeks, while you try to recover from your ordeal? Don't make any rash decisions just yet."

Grace had already mentioned to him about leaving the Church. The Bishop agreed with the vicar's suggestion.

"Take some time off, and we can talk about your future when you are feeling stronger."

She left Liverpool the following morning and returned to her family, who were understandably upset.

"I can't imagine the fear you went through, darling, I hope he didn't manage to…"

Her mother couldn't complete her sentence, But Grace knew exactly what she meant.

"No, he didn't violate me, Mum. No need to worry about that."

Her mother breathed an audible sigh of relief.

"Thank God. Your father and I were so worried."

· · ·

THREE WEEKS LATER, after a talk with the Bishop, Grace agreed to take up a post as a vicar in a small town in Oxfordshire.

"It's a pleasant town—I've visited there myself—and it's been without a vicar for two months. The previous vicar was a woman, but she had to leave due to illness after just a year in the post. The current curate is also a woman, and would be of great help to you in learning the ropes, but has said she doesn't want to become a vicar just yet. It's very quiet and more genteel than your last parish. I'm sure you will feel safe there."

The Bishop smiled broadly, as if he had solved all the problems of the world. Grace was a little more hesitant, but realised she couldn't hide out at her parents' home forever, and must face life again.

So it was that she began work as the vicar of the church in Swinbury, Oxfordshire. The Curate turned out to be a kindly, helpful woman, and the vicarage was a comfortable, modern three-bedroomed house next to the church. Unfortunately, the first duty she had to perform five days after her arrival, was the funeral of a sixteen-year-old schoolgirl, called Charlotte Trent. Grace found the event harrowing; particularly in view of her own recent experience; but she got through it, doing her best to comfort the mother and the boyfriend of a girl who, from the pictures she saw, had been a pretty and popular young woman. The mother, in particular, was totally devastated, and seemed to be in a cataclysmic state of shock. Grace had to dig deep to offer as much support and understanding as possible—both before and after the funeral; visiting the mother several times to offer comfort as best she could.

Grace gradually settled into the small community, and began to learn about some of her parishioners. Whether they attended her church or not; or whether they were even religious, she treated them all the same. She had the ability to draw people's stories out of them. She was genuinely interested in people, and they responded to that. Bumping into Jennifer Blake in the High Street one day, she learned of her former career as a journalist, and about her American partner who had come to join her in retirement in her home town. A month or two later, her curate mentioned Dorinda Lake, a former school teacher, who turned out to be an occasional church goer.

"She killed her mother, and that was very wrong," said the curate, in conversation over a cup of coffee. "But from what I've learned, she was sorely provoked into a moment of madness, and has paid the penalty for it. She's been to the church a few times, and I've chatted briefly with her. She's actually a nice woman."

Grace looked a little shocked to hear that a murderer had been in the church; someone her Curate even described as a nice woman; but knew she must not judge. She would try and speak with her one day. Everyone deserved forgiveness if they were genuinely sorry for what they had done.

"She even has a partner, now." The curate seemed to know all the local gossip. "He's a local builder, who was doing some work on her home. Someone saw them coming from the cinema recently, holding hands."

"Well, I'm pleased for them. I hope the man isn't married, though."

"No, no," came the reply, with a vigorous shaking of the head. He's a widower. His son's girlfriend was the one who was tragically killed, and whose funeral took place a week after you arrived."

Grace's face showed the horror she still felt about that poor girl's death.

"Well I'm glad the family have some good things happening in their lives, after all that tragedy."

She wondered how her curate knew all this, and hoped she wasn't gossiping all the time. Had she had been the subject of any gossip in the town since her arrival? But wasn't bold enough to ask.

DORINDA LAKE

DORINDA WAS glad she had taken the plunge and accepted Arthur's offer of dinner at a local restaurant, about a week after he and Dennis had finished work on the kitchen. He had looked so embarrassed and red-faced as he asked her, that she responded quickly, if only to put him out of his obvious discomfort.

"I'd love to have dinner with you, Arthur. I shall look forward to it."

He had relaxed a little more after his stuttered message had been conveyed.

"Good. I'm pleased."

"You and Dennis have done an absolutely wonderful job with the kitchen. It's modern and bright, but not too high-tech. I'm not really into kitchens that look like the inside of a space station. I'll enjoy cooking in here. You must come and have dinner here, too. Then we can talk about you doing some more work for me."

AFTER THE INITIAL NERVOUSNESS, the two slipped into an easy-going, friendly relationship. Dorinda had been unused to being in male company for much of her life, but found Arthur to be calm and undemanding, and easy company. She had been nervous at first about whether sex would rear its head. She hadn't told Arthur that she was completely inexperienced in such matters; heading for old age and still a virgin. What would he think about that? Would he be shocked? Amused? She had no idea. Maybe that side of things was no longer important to him, and she wasn't sure how she would feel if that were the case. Relief, perhaps? Or would there be a tinge of disappointment that she would never discover the joys of married life? As the weeks progressed in their fledgling relationship, the extent of the passion between them was restricted to hand-holding, and a kiss on the cheek as they said goodnight.

She rarely thought back to her time in prison. It had been quite shocking at first; the noise, the swearing from some of the prisoners, the blandness and boredom of everyday life in that institution. At first, she had been a target for one or two bullies; both inmates and staff. But she drew on her years of teaching and began to stand up for herself, and the bullying stopped. There were some obvious same-sex relationships – quite openly displayed, and she was even targeted by a large, tattooed woman for a while, who turned out to be a gentle, kindly person when Dorinda got to know her. She had explained as sensitively as she was able, that, while she had the greatest respect for women who chose to have intimate relations with other women, she, herself, was not sexually attracted to them. In fact, to be honest, she hadn't been all that attracted to men in that way, either.

In the end, she became liked and respected by many of the women she met, while inside. She taught one or two how to read, and how to write letters. Others would come and ask her advice about family matters, as though Dorinda was some sort of expert in that field. It even amused her that some prisoners wanted advice on sex and relationships, and were utterly amazed when she told them she had never had a relationship. It seemed a whole section of life had completely passed her by, and it didn't look to her as though it would change in the future.

As for her mother, she came to accept that she was wrong to have struck her in the way that she obviously had; not that she had any recollection still of the events of that day. She should have left her mother many years before. However, the past was the past, and there was no point dwelling on it.

Arthur never asked her about what had led to her being imprisoned; nor about her experiences while she was there. He simply wasn't interested in the matter. His thoughts were entirely centred on the present.

Elizabeth was turning out to be a model pupil; always on time, with homework prepared as requested. Dorinda had no doubt she would soon have caught up with her fellow pupils, and be able to take the exams the following summer. Just occasionally she would refer to her life before her transplant, but mostly, like Arthur, she lived in the present.

Dorinda realised that Elizabeth was becoming very fond of Dennis. Even after the work was finished on the kitchen, and the two men had departed to work elsewhere, Dennis would still sometimes turn up to walk home with her, when his work commitments permitted, but Dorinda didn't mention him to the young woman. It really wasn't her place to do so. Instead, she thought more and more of Dennis's father, Arthur.

Arthur was now coming to visit, or taking her out for a meal, around four times weekly. When he visited, she would cook him a plain, but tasty meal, of the kind he favoured. Roast beef was one of his favourites. They usually ate in the now smart and cheerful kitchen, as the dining room was being used for teaching.

"I thought I might have my bedroom re-decorated," she told Arthur one day. "It's looking very dull, and I would like to have some new furniture."

It had been her bedroom while her mother was alive, and although her mother's room was bigger, she didn't want to move into that room after her death. She reserved that room mainly for storage and rarely went in there.

"Let's take a look, and you can tell me what you want."

This was the first time that Arthur had been inside her bedroom. They had been dating for several months by now, but the bedroom issue had never been raised. As they went into the room, Dorinda felt almost embarrassed about how drab it was. Why hadn't she tried to do something about it before? Arthur, however, was very tactful and kind.

"Yes, I see what you mean. But a few coats of paint, and we'll have it fresh and pretty – as pretty as the person who sleeps here."

Dorinda blushed a little. She wasn't used to compliments. Besides, she was anything but pretty, she thought. Arthur realised that she was a little overwhelmed and put his arm around her shoulder to reassure her, and before they knew it, the pair of them were locked into an embrace, before Arthur turned to face her and kissed her full on the lips for the first time.

"Oh," was all Dorinda could say, after the short, but firm kiss.

"I thought it was about time we were a little more romantic. I hope I haven't upset you. It just seemed right, that's all."

"Yes, it did, didn't it? It seemed right to me too."

Then before she lost her courage, she took the initiative and kissed him back.

They stood for a moment, arms still around each other. It was Arthur who broke the silence.

"It just seemed like the right time and the right place." He nodded towards the bed. "But perhaps you're not interested in changing things. Perhaps you're happy with what we have."

He wasn't talking about the décor, however.

Dorinda sat on the edge of the bed, and Arthur placed himself next to her, their thighs touching. She spoke quietly, and a little nervously.

"I know you were married for a long time, and I expect you and your wife had a close relationship…you know…"

She couldn't bring herself to say the words, so Arthur said them for her.

"Yes, we were married for a long time, and yes, we enjoyed normal marital relations for much of that time. But that doesn't mean that we have to have that type of relationship. Don't get me wrong, I find you attractive, and the thought of being in bed, on a cold winter's night, with my arms around you, keeping each other warm, sounds attractive to me. But if it isn't for you, I'll understand." He paused.

The words that came out of Dorinda's mouth next, surprised even her. She had no idea where the boldness came from, but bold she felt.

"Perhaps you would like to spend the night with me soon, and we can see how we like it. Why don't you come over on Saturday night for dinner, and then spend the night here?" She giggled. "My word. Just imagine what my mother would have said if she had heard me inviting a man to stay overnight with me in my bed."

Arthur smiled back, delighted in seeing another side to the woman of whom he was becoming quite fond.

"But she's not here, so it doesn't matter, does it? And yes, I would love to come over Saturday night, and stay over with you."

ALONE AGAIN, Dorinda was alternately excited and scared. What had she done? As Saturday night approached, she felt distinctly strange, nervous in her stomach and worried that it all might go wrong.

The doorbell rang at precisely seven p.m. A smiling Arthur, clutching a bunch of flowers, and wearing his best suit, awaited her.

"These are lovely. Thank you. Come in. Dinner is nearly ready."

"Well if it tastes as good as the smell coming from your kitchen, then I'm in for a treat."

"I've set up a small table in the sitting room. My dining room is now my office and teaching space, as you know; but

I thought the kitchen, as nice as it looks now, was just a little too informal for a special meal."

She ushered Arthur into the cosy sitting room, where a couple of candles burned on the polished oak drop-leaf table, and the table had been laid with the best cutlery and wine glasses.

"My, you have really gone to town. I'm very glad I came dressed accordingly. Can I say, too, that you are looking delightful in the blue dress."

She smiled, accepting the compliment graciously, but not revealing that it was a new purchase for this special night. Not only had she bought a new dress, but had treated herself to some nice underwear. She wasn't sure of the etiquette of whether she would be expected to wear something in bed, or whether Arthur would expect her to sleep *"au naturelle"*, but decided to buy a fancy nightie just in case. Part of her was trembling with nerves, while the other half was excited about what lay ahead. *Oh, God, I hope I don't make a fool of myself.*

Dorinda indicated towards the bottle of red wine, sitting on the table.

"Would you like to pour out some wine, while I bring in the first course?"

After considering all sorts of fancy dishes, she had eventually settled on something simple; prawn cocktail, followed by a beef in red wine casserole. She was a moderately competent cook, and had no fears in that direction. No, it was her lack of skills in the bed department that worried her the most. It was tempting to swig back a few glasses of red, to give her Dutch courage, but decided that sobriety might be the better bet.

. . .

ARTHUR PUT down his knife and fork, and gave a satisfied sigh.

"That was delicious, Dorinda. You're an excellent cook."

She glowed; not being used to personal praise.

"Thank you."

"I know I am a guest, but I insist on coming into the kitchen and helping you clear up. I'm quite domesticated, you know."

Since his wife had died, he had done the bulk of the domestic chores; although Dennis could usually be persuaded to help.

They soon made light work of the dirty dishes, and returned to the sitting room, where Arthur dropped down on to the sofa, patting the seat-cushion next to him.

"Let's relax now, and have a little cuddle."

He was clearly trying to put her at her ease, rather than going in for the sudden lunge technique. Dorinda dropped down next to him, and Arthur put his arm around her shoulder. It seemed the natural thing to do, for her to rest her head on his shoulder.

"This is nice, isn't it? I feel like a young man again; on a date with a lovely lady, and measuring my words so I don't come over as crass or insensitive."

"You're neither of those things, Arthur. You're sensitive and kind, and I feel perfectly relaxed, sitting here with you on the sofa. Just don't expect me to take the lead, however. I am totally inexperienced in these matters, as you know."

"To be honest, Dorinda, I may have been with my wife for many years, but she was, in fact, the only woman with whom

I've been intimate. I know some men like to boast about their conquests, but I have little to boast about. So, you've no need to feel intimidated by your lack of experience."

They sat in a comfortable silence for a few minutes, watching the flickering fire effect on the gas fire; each lost in thought.

Eventually, Arthur suggested that Dorinda might like to use the bathroom first, while he remained in the sitting room.

"Give me a shout when you're in bed."

Dorinda had already hung the pretty, new nightie on the back of the bathroom door, and once she had washed her face and cleaned her teeth, she slipped the soft, silky material over her head. Looking at herself in the full-length mirror, she was satisfied with her reflection. She would never be young and pretty, but for a woman her age she thought she looked good enough.

In the bedroom she switched on just the bedside light, turning off the harsher main light, before pulling back the crisp, clean sheets and climbing into bed. Calling to Arthur, she heard him walk along the landing and go into the bathroom opposite. A few minutes later, he entered the bedroom, closing the door behind him.

That night, Arthur was gentle and considerate. He admired her pretty nightdress, kissed and cuddled her, and made sure she was happy every step of the way. He had had a long and happy sex life with his late wife; but was conscious of how different life had been for Dorinda. At his age, he wouldn't be performing any extraordinary sexual feats anyway; of that he was sure. But he didn't want to disappoint Dorinda in any way.

. . .

As the sun streamed through the bedroom window the following morning, Dorinda awoke to find Arthur sleeping happily beside her. She reflected on the events of the night, and felt a warm glow around her body. She had known, and mentally prepared for the physical aspects of lovemaking; but had been totally unaware of the emotional feelings that might accompany them.

Arthur opened his eyes; aware that Dorinda was watching him. He reached out his hand, and took hers in his.

"Good morning. How are you?"

Dorinda smiled broadly.

"Good morning. I'm wonderful, thank you. Just wonderful."

She drew towards him and kissed him. Life seemed wonderful to her that morning, and that was a feeling she couldn't ever recall having in her life. She realised just how boring and monotonous her life had been, in fact, before meeting Arthur. She would never get back those years she had lost, but was determined to make the most of the ones remaining to her.

CHAPTER 7

G RANT LE FEVRE

DESPITE THE YEARS that had passed since Grant's time in Yemen with the Special Forces, the period had never left his mind. From time to time he had woken with a start, and relived the events of that time; often waking with sweat on his brow and his heart pounding. He had never discussed it with Jennifer, although she had been woken with a start on a few occasions, when Grant had sat bolt upright in bed.

He hadn't kept in close touch with his fellow unit members. He'd been busy in subsequent years travelling the world as a photographer, and now he simply wanted to put that earlier part of his life out of his mind. The problem was, his mind didn't always want to let him forget.

"You want to talk about it?"

He had yelled and sat up in bed, shortly after moving in with Jennifer. Naturally she was concerned, but was reluctant to probe too much, for fear that Grant would resent it.

"Nah! Just a few bad memories. They jump up from time to time. You go back to sleep."

He swung his legs over the side of the bed and stood up.

"Just going for a drink."

He descended the stairs, barefoot, and went into the kitchen, taking the bottle of milk from the fridge and pouring some into a glass.

Thoughts of Danny and Lewis came into his mind. They would have been in late middle-age, like him, if they had lived. After returning to the States, he had visited Danny's wife, and Lewis' mother, to express his condolences. They hadn't asked too many questions, knowing that their husband and son had been involved in a secretive mission, and had seemed reassured that Grant, or Mac as they knew him then, would have done his best for them. But had he? That was the question that constantly came into his mind. Should he have done more to save them? Or would going back have simply meant the sacrifice of a third life? He would probably never know now. But the questions continued to torment him, all these years later.

He had been thoroughly debriefed at the time, and his fellow soldiers, and commanding officer had accepted that he had done all he could to protect his companions. But, in the dark recesses of his mind, he wondered whether there was something more he could have done to save them, and the dark thoughts came back to torment him from time to time.

Jennifer, as a seasoned foreign reporter, had experience of the trauma of war, and was willing to help in any way she could—he knew that—but this was something he kept to himself. He didn't want it tainting their newly-discovered romance, so he endured the occasional bad dream, and hoped they would diminish over time.

He returned to the bedroom, and hoped that Jennifer had fallen asleep again. But she lay, watching him as he climbed back into bed.

"I know you don't want to talk about it to me, and I respect that. But I think you should talk to someone, anyone, before whatever is churning around in your brain begins to cause real damage."

Grant grimaced, even though she probably couldn't see his expression in the dark.

"I'll think about it," was all he said, before turning over, away from her. She sighed and tried to return to sleep.

Next morning, both were a little irritable through lack of sleep, and snapped at each other over breakfast. Eventually, Jennifer braved his wrath to bring up the subject again.

"Grant, we can't keep sweeping things under the table. Sooner or later our pasts can come back to haunt us. If you and I are to stand a chance together, we need to confront stuff like this. I'm on your side. You know that. Please don't shut me out."

Grant reached out with his hand, taking her dainty one in his roughened, masculine palm.

"I'm sorry; you're right. I must try and be more open about these things. It's been a long time buried, and I don't know why it still comes to the surface after all this time. I'll try—I really will."

"Start by telling me the story. What were you doing in Yemen? Back then it was just a godforsaken piece of desert and rocks. It wasn't of interest to anyone; unlike now, when it's being used by other countries to fight a proxy war."

"It was after the communist coup. The US was concerned about the new Republic being aligned with the Soviet bloc. I was sent in with two other men to offer help to the moderates, and to gather intelligence. Unfortunately, someone betrayed us and we were captured by the communist insurgents, who planned to execute us all. But first they tried to extort money from the US government, whose policy was not to give in to blackmail. At first, they denied we were even in the country. We felt utterly alone. Abandoned."

Jennifer's face reflected the concern she had for him, but she said nothing; allowing him to tell his story.

"We knew our only chance was to break out and try to reach the south. We had no weapons, and were only wearing Yemeni clothing; no strong army boots. Danny was the weakest of us. He had been badly beaten when we were caught. Lewis whispered to me that if we broke out, we might be forced to leave Danny behind, or we would all be caught and probably killed immediately. I desperately didn't want to leave anyone behind. It goes against our ethos as soldiers. No one is left behind. But I knew Lewis was telling the truth. If we didn't abandon Danny, it was probable that none of us would survive."

Grant paused for a moment while he poured more coffee for himself. Again, Jennifer remained silent, and, after a few sips of coffee, Grant continued.

"We took advantage of one of the camels breaking free. While our captives were distracted, we made it through the perimeter, and out into the desert. It wasn't long before Danny began to lag behind. I wanted to wait, but even Danny himself said we should go on. So, Lewis and I forged ahead as fast as we could. We heard them capture Danny, and I heard his screams as they beat him again. Eventually, there was a short burst of gunfire, and the screaming stopped. We knew Danny was dead."

Grant paused to sip some more coffee, while Jennifer topped up her cup. When they were both again seated, he began again, unprompted by Jennifer, who let him proceed at his own speed.

"Lewis and I carried on walking. Neither of us spoke— our thoughts on Danny, and our own chances of survival. It was only a couple of miles further on that Lewis fell quite badly. He tripped over a rock in the dark, and the pain made him call out. My instinct was to go to him, but I was sure that the sound of his yell would carry a long distance over the desert. I needed to get as far from him as I could. We had already agreed that each of us must think only of our own survival, if we were to escape, but my heart was so heavy as I walked as fast as I could in my weakened state, to put as much distance between us. That decision was the most painful one of my entire life, and one that has filled me with guilt ever since."

He lowered his face, away from Jennifer's. She put down her coffee and went around the table; standing between his bare feet and pulling his body into hers, so his head rested against her stomach; holding him, in silent sympathy.

Eventually she urged Grant to seek some help.

"We both know that soldiers can suffer from PTSD. There's no shame in seeking help, you know. You've carried this burden around with you for a long time, Grant. Maybe you need help to let it go."

But Grant just shook his head, and smiled wanly.

"It's okay. Don't worry. It doesn't happen very often these days. It's perhaps just the change in my life that's disrupted my mind a little."

Then he changed the subject.

DENNIS MASON

DENNIS AND ELIZABETH had settled into a warm and loving friendship very quickly. They dated three or four times a week, and their closeness was obvious to all around them. Dennis hadn't yet attempted to become intimate, but he felt the time was rapidly coming when they could move their relationship to the next level. He still felt that Elizabeth was keeping something from him, but decided to allow her the time to reveal it, without being pressured by him.

It was one day at the King George V Pub, where a popular local band were playing, that he learned the truth about his girlfriend. A young woman suddenly rushed over to them and flung her arms around Elizabeth.

"Oh wow! Elizabeth. How lovely to see you; you're looking so well these days."

Dennis recognised the girl as Lauren, from school; a loud, somewhat exuberant girl, but with a kind heart. He wondered what she meant by saying that Elizabeth was looking well. Lauren and Elizabeth chatted for a moment, with the former turning and giving Dennis a big smile when

Elizabeth told her they were dating. Eventually, they finished their chat, and, with a smile, Lauren returned to her own friends.

"What did she mean about you looking so well? Have you been ill?"

Elizabeth gave a slight smile.

"I don't want to tell you here. Shall we walk home? I can tell you then."

The band had finished playing, so they left the pub and began the walk back to Elizabeth's home.

"You don't remember me from school?" she asked Dennis.

"No, should I? I told you I would remember a girl as pretty as you."

"Do you remember the girl in the wheelchair? The one who was often missing because of her poor health?"

Dennis stopped, and stared at her.

"That was you? I don't believe it. You look so different. Wow! I don't know what to say."

"I knew you hadn't recognised me right from the start, but I thought you would in time. I didn't realise it would take this long."

"So, you got better? What happened?"

"I have cystic fibrosis. My lungs were packing up, and I was getting close to dying. Then I was so lucky. I was able to have a heart and lung transplant. It saved my life."

For a few seconds Dennis's mind didn't process what he had just heard, but, without warning, Elizabeth's words echoed around his brain. He was having trouble breathing; his breaths coming in short, sharp pants. *Surely she didn't... surely it's not...* He couldn't process the thoughts now in his head. He felt a little dizzy, and grabbed on to a lamp-post.

Elizabeth stopped too, a little concerned about the effect her pronouncement had had on him.

"What's the matter, Dennis? Are you feeling okay?"

Dennis's face was white, as he asked her the question.

"What date did you have the transplant?"

She told him, and his heart nearly stopped.

It was the day that Charlotte had died.

REALISING the impact her words were having on Dennis, Elizabeth now knew. She knew the identity of the mystery donor who had given her a second chance of life. It was Dennis's former childhood sweetheart. She reached out her hand to touch Dennis.

"Oh, God, Dennis. I never suspected…I mean…they never tell you about the donor. I just felt so bad for his or her family. They never even said that it was a girl. I had no idea."

She realised that Dennis had had a severe shock, and reached out to give him a hug, but he pulled away from her, before turning and resting his hands on a brick wall; deep in thought as he processed the information.

Finally, he turned back to her, and saw her distressed face.

"I'm sorry. The shock…it's hard to take it in. Let's go."

He took Elizabeth's hand as they continued their walk, but there was no conversation. It had been killed stone dead by the news. When they reached Elizabeth's house he simply bent and kissed her briefly on the cheek.

"I have to go. I need to think. I'm sorry…"

His voice tailed off, as a tearful Elizabeth turned and went inside.

. . .

ARTHUR WAS HOME THAT NIGHT. It wasn't his night to stay with Dorinda, and, seeing his son's face, he was glad of that.

"What's up lad? You look as though you've seen a ghost."

At that, his son burst into tears.

"Oh God, Dennis, what's happened."

He moved towards his only son and embraced him; something he hadn't done in a long while. When Dennis stopped crying, they both sat down at the kitchen table while Dennis told him of the night's events.

"That must have been a shock to learn that. Did Elizabeth know beforehand? Was she keeping it from you? Or was it a shock for her too?"

For the first time, Dennis felt bad about leaving Elizabeth so abruptly. He was sure that it was complete news to her. It must have been as big a shock to her as to him. Arthur reassured him.

"Don't worry, lad. I'll ring and make sure she's alright."

Dennis heard him on the phone, probably talking to Elizabeth's Dad. He returned after a moment.

"It's alright. She's okay. I explained that it was a shock, and that's why you had left so quickly. Her Dad say she will take care of her."

He returned to comforting his son.

"I expect it's brought it all back; you know, the accident and that. What a terrible coincidence. I don't suppose it ever crossed the mind of either of you. Do you want to talk about it, lad, or would you prefer to get some sleep and perhaps talk in the morning?"

"I think I'll just go to my room, if you don't mind, Dad."

. . .

IN THE PRIVACY of his room, Dennis cried a little more; tears that maybe should have been shed after Charlotte had died, but which had remained trapped in his body, and only now released when he heard from Elizabeth about her transplant. It seemed an almost impossible coincidence that the heart beating inside his current girlfriend, was the same one he had heard beating inside his former one. What were the odds of something so strange happening like that?

He tossed and turned all night—thoughts of both Charlotte and Elizabeth passing through his mind. Had the discovery changed the way he felt about Elizabeth. Would it be too weird if he had sex with her at some future point, knowing that Charlotte's heart was beating in her body? It sounded crazy, but would Charlotte be jealous? He woke the following morning, feeling exhausted. Thankfully it was Saturday, so there was no work to get up for. He knew he should go and see Elizabeth and talk about things. The poor girl must be tormented too, he was sure.

His Dad was sitting in the kitchen when he went down, and looked up from the newspaper he had been reading. He looked at his son with compassion.

"How are you doing? Manage to sleep?"

Dennis grunted an acknowledgement, reinforced with a nod. He wasn't the best conversationalist first thing in the morning; even less now after so little sleep. Arthur waited until he had made some coffee before he spoke again.

"Will you go to see Elizabeth this morning? I think you should, for both your sakes."

Denis sat at the table; the steaming mug of coffee

between both hands, which was still too hot to drink. Feeling the heat on his fingers he put it down on to the table.

"Yes, I think I should. But I don't know what to say, really. It's such a weird situation."

"It is, lad, but talking about it might help. Think of it like this; Charlotte, who you loved, has gone. She can never return. But she left you a wonderful gift. She gave life to another girl. A girl you have come to care about. Maybe, in a strange kind of way, it's a sign that she approves of your choice."

Dennis sighed a little, but did not reply. Perhaps his Dad was right? Elizabeth was an innocent party in all this. It wouldn't be right for him to somehow blame her for anything. He was so confused right now.

An hour later he was heading over to Elizabeth's house. Her Dad answered the door, and smiled sympathetically. He and Dennis had always got along. He didn't want to see either of the youngsters in pain.

"She's upstairs in her room. She's up though. Go up if you like."

Dennis tapped nervously at her bedroom door, and Elizabeth opened it. They took one look at each other's sad faces and began to hug. Elizabeth stepped back into the room, and pulled Dennis with her, before shutting the door with her foot, as Dennis stepped away once more.

"It's okay. Come and listen to her heart. I know you want to."

Dennis hesitated at first. Did he really want to? But his instinct was to move forwards. He placed his ear next to Elizabeth's chest and heard the steady throb of Charlotte's heart. He couldn't help himself, as the tears flowed down his cheek once more. Elizabeth just held him close and stroked his hair. They stood in silence for several moments.

"Come and sit down."

Dennis sat down next to her on the bed.

"I was so happy when I received this heart. It meant I could live again. But I am even happier now that I know it was given by someone you loved; someone you probably still love, I hope. I can't replace her, I know that. But while I'm alive, a part of her still lives. Do you think that too?"

Dennis collected his thoughts.

"Yes, you're right. She lives on a little through you. I'm sorry I left so quickly last night. It was just the shock...you know I never gave any thought to the person who had been given her heart. It was just an anonymous person somewhere. But thinking about it now, I'm so glad it was given to you. If you had both died, I would have lost you both; even though I barely knew you back then. It's as though fate has led us to each other."

He put his arm around her shoulder and kissed her gently on the lips. They wouldn't make love today. Maybe not even for a while. But he knew they would, in time. And he was happy about that.

CHAPTER 8

OREEN TRENT

DOREEN TRENT'S life had almost ended when that of her daughter, Charlotte's, ended. She began to drink. Just a few glasses at first. But within a few months it had taken control of her life. It just seemed easier to face the day somehow, after a glass of wine with breakfast—or even instead of breakfast. She told her Doctor that she was depressed, but didn't mention that she was drinking. The pills prescribed by the doctor didn't help very much, but she took them anyway, as well as the drink. Life became a blur.

She had no close relatives. It had only been her and Charlotte, after her husband had walked out. He'd never kept in touch with them, and refused to send any money to support them, so Doreen didn't even bother to let him know that

Charlotte had been killed. Whether he found out by other means, she had no idea, and cared even less. Last she heard of him, some five years earlier, he had been living with a woman in the next town, and had fathered two children with her.

Charlotte had been her whole life. All her ambitions for the future had been channelled through her pretty daughter. Almost losing her at five had been bad enough. But to have it happen again – for real this time – drove a jackhammer through her heart. Charlotte's boyfriend, Dennis, had come to see her a couple of times after the accident, but Doreen found it hard to even make conversation with him. It wasn't that she blamed him for her daughter's death, but if she hadn't been with him…the consequence was obvious as far as she was concerned. Dennis stopped calling. In fact, everyone stopped calling.

She went out twice weekly to the supermarket to buy food; some of which she ended up throwing in the trash. After a bottle of wine, food didn't seem quite so important. She didn't drive, so would pull her trolley full of food, with several bottles of wine in the bottom, up the slope leading to her house, with some difficulty. But there was no one to assist, so she had to continue to struggle; even leaving the trolley outside in the rain once, when she had drunk rather more than usual. Neighbours who saw her tutted, but didn't offer to help. There were times when Doreen even contemplated ending it all. Life really wasn't worth the effort she concluded.

It was Grace Bennett, the vicar, who eventually came to her aid. Seeing her walking along past the church one day, pulling her trolley behind her, she asked her curate, the fount of all the local knowledge, who she was, and was shocked to find that she was the mother of the young girl for whom she had performed her first funeral after arriving in the parish. Although she had visited her a few times after the funeral, it had been a while since she had seen her, and Grace noted the difference between how she looked then, and today. After chatting to her for a moment, she invited her into the vicarage for a cup of tea. To her surprise, Doreen, accepted.

"Here, have a biscuit with your tea."

Doreen hesitated, but then accepted. It had been a long time since anyone offered her a kindness.

"Thank you."

"I'm sorry I didn't recognise you at first. It was only when my curate pointed out that you are Charlotte's mother."

At the mention of her daughter's name, Doreen raised her face and looked at the vicar. She hadn't recognised her either, from that day when she attended the funeral of her only child, and the few visits afterwards. It had only been the liquor consumed beforehand that had got her through the service. As for who was present, she had no idea. She didn't respond verbally, so Grace continued to chat.

"I'm sorry I haven't seen you since that time. You must have been through such an ordeal. I hope you know that you can call on me at any time for a cup of tea and a chat. I would be happy to call on you again, too."

"Thank you," was Doreen's eventual reply. I don't talk to many people. "I just go out for the food shopping on Monday and Thursday. Rest of the time I stay home."

Her hands were a little shaky, but she managed to hold the cup and saucer without spilling any tea, or dropping it, which she had done once or twice at home. She wasn't sure why the vicar had invited her into her home, but it was a kind gesture.

"Have you thought about coming to church on Sundays, sometimes? The congregation here are very kind. We get together after the morning service for a cup of coffee and a chat, in the church hall."

Doreen looked surprised by the invitation. Since losing Charlotte, life had pretty much lost all meaning, and she had lost any inclination to make friends with anyone. However, she was touched by the kindness of the young vicar.

"Thank you. Perhaps I will one Sunday."

"Tell me about Charlotte; if that's not too painful for you."

It took a few moments for Doreen to gather her thoughts. But eventually, in a quiet voice, she began to talk.

"She was my only child. Her father left us when she was quite young. She was so pretty. Everyone said so. I nearly lost her when she was five. She came close to being hit by a speeding car in the High Street. Perhaps that was an omen."

Grace's eyes exuded sympathy. This poor woman had truly suffered.

"We don't know why God chooses to take some of us back home earlier than others. Some find it easier to think about what they had rather than what they have lost. You had your beautiful daughter for sixteen years, when you might only have had her for five. As hard as this is to accept, it is another way to think about her."

"I can't believe in a God who takes a sweet, innocent child, who has caused no harm to anyone, and yet leaves some truly evil people in the world, untouched."

Grace reached out and took her hand, giving it a light squeeze.

"I can understand that. It is so difficult to accept losses like your daughter. It must have devastated your life. How have you coped?"

"I haven't," said Doreen simply. My life stopped when Charlotte breathed her last breath. I exist, but I don't live. Sometimes I think I should end it all. What is the point of me carrying on?"

"You might think like that now. But maybe it won't always be like that. Would Charlotte want you to spend your whole life grieving over her? One day you might be able to think about her without so much pain. Perhaps you could even find something to fill your life again—something as a tribute to your daughter; to let the world remember she was here, and was loved? Time changes many things. Don't give up too easily. If you want friendship, come along to the church and join one of our organisations. You may find it a comfort in your grief."

THAT NIGHT, Doreen Trent, for the first time since her daughter's death, didn't open a bottle of wine, and slept a more peaceful sleep than for a while.

JENNIFER AND GRANT

JENNIFER AND GRANT settled down into a comfortable, cosy existence—as though they had lived together for many years. They shared the household chores and the food shopping, and enjoyed cooking together in the kitchen that Jennifer had modernised after her parent's deaths. One would cook one night, while the other sat on a counter stool, sipping wine, and would swap roles the next night. They chatted about the events of the day—both personal and national. With their news gathering backgrounds, they were both still interested in all the major issues of the day—agreeing on most things; and agreeing to differ on others.

Both had begun to write—fiction for Jennifer, and an autobiography for Grant. They had a corner each of what had been a spare bedroom, and which Jennifer had furnished with a couple of antique desks, and some bookshelves. Grant professed himself delighted with it.

"I thought your house was next to the river?" He was looking out of the window at the time, and remembering the tragic drowning of Jennifer's twin, many years earlier. He didn't think she would mind being reminded of the event.

"It was. But about twenty years ago, they diverted it to stop flooding. It is about half a mile from here now."

"That's good. I'm glad you don't have to continually see it."

Jennifer came to stand beside him, looking out of the window. Where the river had been was now a development of retirement homes, well planted with trees between the homes. It was a quiet part of the town, and the traffic was very small. She was glad she had kept the house now. She had long come to terms with her twin's drowning, but was glad she didn't have to continually look at the place where it had happened.

Grant put his arm around her shoulder.

"Thank you for letting me share your beautiful home. I'm very happy to be here."

He bent his head and kissed her gently on the lips.

"And I'm happy you're here too. We're going to make this work, Grant. I know we are. Now, what I want to know is who will be the first to get a book published?"

"Ah! That is the question. I guess we had better get to work."

THEY SETTLED INTO AN EASY GROOVE – writing each morning, and spending the afternoons gardening, or travelling the local countryside, eating out in country pubs, with the occasional day trip to London, when the yearning came for theatre performances, or music concerts, not available in their part of Oxfordshire. Contentment ruled in both their lives.

Unfortunately, the idyll came to an end one day, with a ghost of Grant's past reappearing. Sitting at her desk, Jennifer glanced out of the window, and was surprised to see a man standing by the gate, looking into the garden. He looked up at the window and caught her looking down at him, and immediately moved out of view, behind the privet hedge. She turned back to her laptop, and thought no more about it.

However, an hour later, she saw the same man through the bedroom window, which overlooked the back of the house. He was walking very slowly up the garden, and keeping close to the hedge.

"Grant. Come here. There's a suspicious-looking character in the back garden."

Grant came quickly from the study next door, and was

just in time to see the man before he was hidden by the greenhouse. His face had turned white, Jennifer noticed.

"What's the matter, Grant? Who is it?"

Grant's voice was a little strained.

"It's been a long time, but it looks like…no, it can't be."

He dashed from the room, calling behind him.

"Stay here. If you don't hear from me in five minutes, call the police."

Then he was gone. She heard him running down the stairs, and towards the back door, which, thankfully, was kept locked all the time nowadays, unlike when she was a child in the house. All went quiet for a few moments. She began to tremble. Something horrible was going to happen; she was certain.

GRANT PAUSED behind the back door, straining to hear any noise from the other side. He looked sideways towards the window, trying to see if there was a human shadow in view. He'd only seen the man for a brief moment. *Surely it couldn't be him? After all these years?* The figure he had seen bore a strong resemblance to Lewis; the US Special Forces soldier he thought had died in Yemen; albeit aged quite a lot.

Grant had kept himself pretty fit since those days. But even so, he was no longer in the prime of life. If it *was* Lewis, he was sure he wasn't paying a friendly call; especially not creeping towards the house in the way he was. It seemed to him that Lewis would be only be there for malevolent reasons. Grant didn't have a gun licence in the UK. They had much tighter regulations for owning firearms than back home. Besides, he had always felt very safe here. There was no reason to own a gun.

He glanced around the kitchen for a suitable weapon, should one be needed; his eyes settling on the knife-block on the granite surface near the cooker. But to get there he would have to risk being seen through the large window. If this man was Lewis, and was carrying a gun...

His thoughts were interrupted by the ring of the front door bell. Surely, he couldn't have made it around to the front door so quickly. He backed slowly into the hallway, and saw Jennifer standing fearfully at the top of the stairs.

"Look through the window," he whispered to her. "See who's there."

She looked through the landing window and turned back to Grant with a surprised expression on her face.

"It's the vicar. The woman vicar. I've seen her once or twice as I've walked past the church. What the heck is she doing here?"

GRACE BENNETT (One hour earlier)

GRACE SAW the man sitting in the churchyard again. He was dressed in the same shabby jacket and sneakers. He'd been there the previous day, but when she had gone to talk to him, he had disappeared. Today, however, he remained seated on the bench as she approached.

"Hello. I saw you here yesterday. Do you need any help?"

The man looked up at her, but his eyes looked blank—devoid of expression. Grace tried again.

"My name's Grace Bennett. I'm the vicar here. What's your name?"

This time the man responded in a flat voice. "It's Lewis."

"Hello Lewis. You don't sound like a local. Where are you from?"

"I'm from Chicago. USA," he added, as if she might not know where Chicago was."

"Well you're a long way from home. Are you here on holiday?"

"I'm looking for someone."

"Someone who lives here; in the town?"

"I've been told he does. Name of Mac. From the States too."

Grace thought for a moment, then shook her head.

"I can't say I know anyone called Mac, or who speaks with an American accent. Of course, he may not be a church-goer. Is he a friend of yours?"

The man gave a cynical laugh.

"Not exactly. I've been searching for him for a long time. I rather hoped he would be dead by now."

Grace looked a little startled. Although the man had made no threatening gestures towards her, she felt the same dread as she had felt in Liverpool, about the man who had attacked her. Her stomach felt heavy with dread. Nevertheless, she thought she needed to continue the conversation, but was nervous that she had forgotten to slip her phone into her pocket, and that she was alone in the vicarage; the curate having a day off today.

"Would you like to tell me about it? Why are you looking for him?"

Lewis gave her a strange look, but declined to answer her questions.

"Not right now. I've been told where he may be living. I'll go and see if he's there. You'll hear about it soon enough."

His words sounded a little ominous to Grace. But what could she do? If she called the police every time she spoke to someone a little strange—well, she would be on the phone several times a week. Being a vicar seemed to attract the strange and the dispossessed, it seemed. They looked for someone to talk to, and often the clergy were the only ones they found to listen. This man was clearly disturbed about something, but she had no evidence that he meant any harm to anyone.

Lewis stood up and turned away from her. Against her better judgement, she called after him.

"Won't you come and have a cup of tea with me before you go? Or coffee perhaps?" suddenly realising he was an American, and unused to British tea-drinking habits. But he ignored her and walked away.

He had gone perhaps one hundred yards and Grace felt an overwhelming urge to follow him. She had an ominous feeling about the man. She began walking at the same speed as him; careful to keep a safe distance between them. Lewis did not turn around once as they walked. She saw him turn into the road which had newish retirement homes on one side, and older homes on the other. It was where the river used to flow, so she had been told on her arrival in the town.

By the time she reached the end of that road, he had disappeared from sight. She deduced that he must have turned into the entrance to perhaps the third or fourth house. She went down the drive of the third house and cautiously around the back of the house, but there was no sight of him. Then she caught a brief glance of a man's head through the dividing hedge. He appeared to have stopped.

Walking quickly next door, she went to the front door and rang the bell. She could see a woman looking down from a window above, and the shadow of a man in the front hallway, through the small pane in the door. The door opened, and without waiting for an invitation, she stepped quickly inside, surprising the man holding the door.

"Shut the door. Quickly. There is a man at the back of the house. You may think I'm crazy, but you may be in danger."

The man in the hallway didn't seem surprised by what she was saying. It appeared that he was aware of the man's presence too. She quickly recounted the small amount of information she knew about the man, including his name.

"Lewis? You're sure he said Lewis?"

"Yes, absolutely. He said he was looking for someone called Mac."

"That's me. He's looking for me. He knows me as Mac. My real name is Grant."

The woman on the landing had now run down the stairs and grabbed Grant by the arm.

"We must call the police, Grant. What if he has a weapon?"

Grant didn't have time to respond, before a loud knock came on the front door, and the shape of a man appeared through the small glass pane. He didn't wait for them to respond to his knock; instead calling out.

"You in there, Mac? Someone told me you lived around here. I've been looking for you for a long time. You hid yourself very well. Wouldn't have thought you were the suburban-living sort of a guy."

Grant instinctively pushed both women behind him, towards the kitchen and the back door.

"I'll keep him talking. You call the police, Jennifer, and then the two of you make a run for it through the back."

Turning back to the door, he engaged verbally with Lewis for the first time.

"Lewis? It's really you? I thought you were…"

"Yeah, you thought I was dead, didn't you? Like Danny. Well I'm not. I'm here, and I want to talk to you."

Grace took hold of Jennifer's hand and pulled her from the hallway into the kitchen.

"Is there another way out of the garden through the back door?"

Jennifer responded, in a whisper, but her eyes were still on Grant.

"Yes. There's a gap in the hedge. It takes you into the garden that backs on to mine, and from there on to the next road. But I'm not leaving Grant."

Grant heard his name mentioned and turned towards them.

"You get out, Jennifer. I'll handle Lewis."

Jennifer grabbed her phone from the kitchen table and, reluctantly, followed Grace to the back door, pressing the emergency number as she went.

CHAPTER 9

$\mathcal{G}$RANT LE FEVRE & LEWIS HILL

ONCE HE HAD SEEN the two women head out of the back door, Grant turned his attention back to Lewis, who had remained standing by the front door. He could hear murmuring, but couldn't tell what he was saying, and he seemed very disturbed. Grant decided to talk to him, if only to distract him and stop him from going around the back of the house again and seeing the two women escaping.

"Lewis. It's been a long time. I honestly thought you were dead. When you fell over that rock, I was sure they would soon capture you, and that you would suffer the same fate as Danny."

There was a short pause; then Lewis responded to him.

"They did catch me. They roughed me up pretty bad. But for some reason they didn't kill me. They wanted to use me as bait. To lure more of our guys into coming after us. But they didn't come after us, did they, Mac. They abandoned us."

"Lewis, I'm so sorry for what you went through. You know I would have helped you if I could. I had no weapon. We decided, didn't we? You, me and Danny. We decided that we should each concentrate on our own escape. You remember that, don't you?"

The man outside the door began rambling again. Grant couldn't understand a word he was saying. *Where the heck had he been all these years?*

"Why are you here, Lewis? Why have you been searching for me?"

There was a pause, before the man outside responded.

"I wanted to see if your life had been better than mine. Because mine, frankly, has been a pile of shit. Three of us went into that godforsaken country. Danny died. I might as well have died. But you—you've had a good life, I'm told. A news photographer, I've heard; winning awards. And now retirement to a quiet town in England. Do you want to know what they did to me, Mac? They held me for eight years. Eight fucking years. They tortured me. They starved me. They threatened to kill me so many times, and frankly, I wish they had."

Grant didn't reply immediately. He was stunned by what he had heard. He had told his bosses back in the US that he was sure Lewis would be dead. But, clearly, he wasn't. He felt sick to his stomach. He'd felt some survivor's guilt for many years. But now…now…hearing what this man had endured, he didn't know what to think. If his bosses back home had sent a team in to retrieve the two bodies, and it all went wrong, the repercussions would have been enormous. They weren't supposed to be there in the first place. If they had believed that one of the men was still alive, would they have sent a team in then? Grant hoped they would have, but wasn't sure it would have happened. As sickening as it was to now think, he wasn't sure his countrymen would have gone in after one man, who they thought was already dead. Should he have put pressure on his bosses to bring back the bodies? Was he responsible for what had happened to Lewis? He was tormented. Did he owe this man something?

His legs felt weak, and he sank down the wall of the hallway, and sat on the polished wood floor.

"How can I help you, Lewis? What can I do?"

"There's nothing anyone can do. I can't get back those years. I'm dying, Mac. Cancer. I just wanted to find you. I don't know what I wanted. Revenge? To tell you my story, perhaps? I don't know. I wanted to kill you at one time, you know. For many years I was obsessed with killing you. To make you pay for those years of freedom you had, that I didn't. But now, I just don't know what I want. It's all too late, anyway."

"Are you armed, Lewis? My partner has called the police. They may well send armed cops."

"Nah. No gun. I have a knife. I was going to stab you in the heart and watch you die."

Grant was struggling with his emotions. He didn't fear this man. At first, he had. But not now. The fear had disappeared. Now he just felt intense sorrow, for the pain and suffering he had endured. He wanted to help him somehow.

He knew the police would be there shortly. The thing he most wanted to avoid was Lewis pretending to be armed, and goading the police into shooting him. Grant made a decision, and prayed it was the right one.

"I want you to drop the knife on to the floor, Lewis. Then I will open the door. We can talk. Will you do that?"

A moment of silence followed, before Grant heard the crash of a metal blade on to the garden path. He slowly opened the door, holding his breath as he did. The man facing him was pale and looked a good ten years older than he should. He was thin; his cheeks a little gaunt.

"I'm so sorry, Lewis. So desperately sorry for all that happened to you. But killing me won't bring back those lost years. I would do anything to wind back the clock."

The two men stood looking at each other for a moment; each lost in thought. Lewis spoke first, in a hoarse, emotionally charged voice.

"I know you would, Mac. I know I shouldn't be blaming you for what happened to me. I guess, if the positions had been reversed, I would have done the same. I've been tormented all these years, looking for someone to blame, and wanting some sort of retribution. You were a convenient person to blame, but I was wrong. Killing you wouldn't bring me any sort of peace – I know that deep down."

Without another word his face crumpled and he fell into Grant's arms, sobbing. Grant too couldn't hold back the tears. They were still clutching each other when two police cars, blue light flashing and sirens sounding, pulled up with a screech outside the gate. Two armed policemen crouched beside the front of the car, and called "Armed police."

Grant acted quickly, and kicked the knife under the nearby bush.

"It's okay. Don't shoot. There's no weapons here."

IT TOOK an hour before the police left, after Grant had assured them he was not in harm's way, and that Lewis had simply come to talk and not to threaten him. Lewis was searched and no weapon was found. They decided no offence had been committed.

"He needs medical help," said Grant, out of earshot of Lewis. "I'll make sure he gets it."

Grace and Jennifer returned to the house—Jennifer in tears of relief after she heard that all was well. Grace left in one of the police cars, whose driver said they would give her a ride home.

Once they were all gone, except her, Grant and Lewis, Jennifer clutched Grant's arm.

"I was so frightened. Thank goodness nothing happened. What happens now."

Lewis was, by now, sitting in the living room, drinking a mug of coffee, and looking completely drained.

"I need to make some calls. You stay with Lewis."

He went into the kitchen and took out his phone, which was full of contact details, collected over the years. He made a few calls, then came back into the living room.

"Lewis, I'm going to drive us up to London. I've spoken to a private doctor, and he will see you tonight. I want you to stay at the hospital tonight at least; and longer if necessary. Is that okay?"

Lewis looked blankly at him.

"I have no money."

"That's no problem. I'll take care of it.

A few hours later, the two men were in a small, private hospital. Doctor Jonathan Blake, a cancer specialist, was waiting to see them, as promised. He examined Lewis, while Grant waited in a small lounge nearby. He called Grant back into the room, where Lewis was lying, exhausted, on the bed. He looked up as Grant returned.

"Tell him, doc. I've nothing to hide."

"Very well." He turned to Grant. "Lewis is regrettably correct that the cancer is probably terminal, although I will confirm this with some scans in the morning. There are drugs available, however, that look promising, to hold up the progress of the disease. I may be able to delay it for a year; perhaps longer. As you are aware, he has sustained some mental trauma, and, from the scars on his body, a lot of physical trauma too. I don't know all the details, but I assume you are aware of this?"

"Yes. We served in the US military together. Lewis was captured and tortured while we were on a mission. It happened a long time ago, and I thought he was dead, until he turned up today."

Both men turned to look at Lewis, who had fallen asleep.

"I will admit him for a few days, and we can do some tests, and prescribe any drugs necessary. Will you come back to see him?"

"Yes, sure. I will do what I can for him. I'll go home now, and return tomorrow, late morning."

.   .   .

As HE ENTERED THE HOUSE, Jennifer was sitting in the living room, listening to some music. She jumped up at the sound of the door, and Grant told her what had happened at the hospital.

She rushed into Grant's arms, clutching him tightly.

"I was so frightened."

He kissed her tenderly on the forehead.

"I know you were, honey. I have to admit, I was too, for a while. But when he began crying outside the front door, I knew things would be okay. Thank goodness the cops didn't press any charges."

Jennifer knew what effect Lewis's appearance may have had on him; especially knowing about the flashbacks and bad dreams Grant had suffered over the years. She knew about survivor's guilt, and how it was often found in surviving victims of terrorist attacks, and in the military after dangerous missions where comrades had been lost. She hoped this episode wouldn't add to his mental stress, and decided to broach the subject there and then.

"You did nothing wrong, Grant. You mustn't think you were to blame for what happened to him. The people who did that to him are the guilty people—and maybe your commanding officers should have tried harder to locate him to be certain that he was dead, as you had thought. You did what you had to do, and what he would have done too, if the positions had been reversed."

Grant didn't reply, but held her a little tighter, as they sat, sipping a late-night whisky on the sofa. Maybe she was right, but his brain would need time to process these events.

. . .

DOREEN TRENT

DOREEN TRENT HAD BEEN a different woman after she began attending church on a regular basis. She had also begun attending meetings for people like her who had become a little too dependent on drink. She knew she would never get over the death of her daughter, but was convinced now that alcohol was not the answer. Grace, the vicar, had become a firm friend, and Doreen helped her out in any way she could. Sometimes she would just stay behind after the service and help to tidy up the prayer books. At other times she would make some soup or a casserole, and take it to the vicarage, convinced that Grace didn't eat healthily enough.

"You're very kind," Grace told her, after being presented with a panful of home-made vegetable soup she was convinced was enough for six people.

"I'm only replacing one kindness for another. I miss cooking for someone. Charlotte used to love my soups."

She could mention her daughter's name now, without breaking into tears.

"You must be lonely there on your own. Have you thought of perhaps taking in a lodger? Someone to talk to and cook for?"

"Oh, I'm not sure about that. It would be strange having someone else in the house. I'd have to think about that."

Grace didn't pursue the matter. The seed had been planted, and she would have to wait to see if it germinated. She was happy that Doreen had turned a corner in her grief. That would do for now. But, perhaps, in the future…

. . .

DOREEN'S first major hurdle came when she decided to pack up Charlotte's clothes and give them to a charity shop. It would be so hard, parting with her darling daughter's pretty clothes, but simply having them hanging in her room, gathering dust, wasn't something she wanted. It would be easy to leave the room as it was; a shrine. But she didn't want that. She was sure that Charlotte wouldn't have wanted that either. So, she set to and placed all her daughter's clothes in black bin bags, before ringing a charity to ask if they would collect them.

The woman at the charity she had chosen—an animal charity, as Charlotte had adored animals—was sympathetic, when Doreen had told her why she was donating the clothes.

"I'm so sorry for your loss, Mrs Trent. I will make sure that the clothes are sent to one of our charity shops well away from your town. That way you will be unlikely to see someone wearing your daughter's clothes."

Doreen hadn't considered that and was glad of the woman's thoughtfulness. Once the clothes had gone, she thought again about Grace's suggestion about having a lodger. Perhaps she would get the room decorated, and give the matter further thought. She wondered if Dennis, Charlotte's former boyfriend, and his Dad, would consider decorating the room. Or would that be too weird, she thought? She continued removing the remainder of Charlotte's belongings; the most precious ones to her own room, and the remainder, such as books and trinkets, into bags for the local charity shop, before contacting Arthur Mason and asking him if he would pop round and talk to her about decorating the room.

"If Dennis would rather not work with you on this, I'll understand."

"I'll ask him, Mrs Trent. Actually, it's a small room, isn't it? I can manage quite easily on my own. It will only take a couple of days, so I could probably pull it in next week."

A month later, the room was unrecognisable. It had been transformed from the bedroom of a teenage girl, into a smart and comfortable room for a guest – or maybe a lodger? She hadn't finally decided on that.

LEWIS HILL

LEWIS BEGAN to regain some strength, as the new drugs enabled him to digest his food, and not be continually throwing up as he had before. Grant had visited several times in the two weeks he spent in the hospital, to see how he was.

As well as the new cancer drug, Lewis had been having some psychiatric care; talking daily to a middle-aged doctor about the demons in his mind. He was even able to joke about it to her.

"As the doctor has only promised me another year, I don't suppose it matters too much what the state of my mind is for longer than that."

The doctor smiled. "I can't promise you a longer life, I'm afraid. But if you can have a more peaceful existence, you can enjoy what time is left to you."

She never promised what she couldn't deliver, and to promise false hope to a dying man was something she would not do. Maybe he would have a miraculous recovery; she didn't know. But, in her years of experience, she hadn't known any.

"Have you decided what you will do when you leave here?"

"I guess I will go back to the US; although I have no-one there to go back to, except my daughter; and I haven't seen her for a long time."

GRANT ASKED him the same question when he visited the following afternoon, and wasn't happy when he heard Lewis's response.

"Why don't you stay here then? I can't promise you a home with Jennifer and me, but I'm sure we could find you somewhere to stay in Swinbury. Then we would be close by to help out when needed, and we would do all we can to make your time comfortable."

"That sounds good. I need to raise some money, some-how, to start paying you back for the medical expenses."

"No need. I've been in touch with an army charity. They've agreed to fund eighty per cent of your expenses. I will pay the rest. You will be able to collect your army pension over here, and that will pay for your rent and living expenses. Anything else you need, I will pay."

Grant was relieved to hear that. To think he once wanted to hear that this man was dead; blaming him for all that had happened to him. Now they had become friends.

HE RECEIVED a telephone call from Grant the following day.

"Hey, buddy, good news. I've spoken to the vicar, and one of her parishioners has a room available to let out at a reasonable rate. Why don't I pick you up from the hospital on Friday, when they discharge you, and bring you down here? If this room isn't suitable, then you can stay with us for a couple of days until we find somewhere else."

So it was that, on Friday afternoon, both men stood inside the recently painted room, that had once been occupied by a teenage Charlotte Trent. A slightly nervous Doreen Trent stood at the doorway to the room, as the men cast their eye over it.

"I hope you like it. I tried to make it unfussy – suitable for a man or for a woman. I didn't think you would want wallpaper with roses on, for example."

"Ma'am, it's perfect. Thank you. I'm honoured that you would let out the room that was your late daughter's, to a guy like me. I hear you're not a bad cook either."

Doreen blushed a little shyly.

"Thank you. I expect the vicar has been talking to people about my cooking. If what I cook isn't to your liking, I would be glad to make changes."

"That won't be necessary, ma'am. I'm not a fussy eater."

He turned to Grant.

"This will be fine, Mac. Thank you for your support."

Grant touched his arm, lightly.

"No problem, buddy. No problem at all.

$\mathcal{D}$ENNIS & ELIZABETH

AFTER THE SHOCK of discovering that Charlotte had been Elizabeth's organ donor, Dennis soon became used to the fact that part of his former sweetheart lived on in Elizabeth. He guessed that some people would find it weird; maybe even a little macabre; so they decided not to mention it to people, unless they were asked directly, and they thought it unlikely. The only people, apart from them, who knew about it, were their two fathers.

For a while, they refrained from too much intimacy, even though they both wanted to take their relationship to the next level. It just never seemed the right opportunity, somehow. However, one Saturday night at Dennis' home, when Arthur had gone to spend the night at Dorinda's, as he was doing increasingly these days, and Tom, Elizabeth's father, was away, visiting his brother further north, Dennis asked Elizabeth if she would like to spend the night with him, and she had shyly accepted.

When she arrived, Dennis carried her bag up to his bedroom, where he had made an extra effort to tidy and clean up.

"I've ordered some pizza for us. That okay with you?"

"Sounds great. Thank you."

They went back downstairs, and switched on the TV to watch a film. The pizza arrived part-way through the film, so they ate it from the box in the living room. Dennis was glad that Elizabeth was a relaxed, take-life-as-it-comes kind of girl. She clearly didn't place great importance on expensive restaurant meals, or wanting to sit and eat pizza at the kitchen table. That suited him just fine.

He tried hard not to compare Elizabeth with Charlotte. They were different people, despite now having the same heart and lungs. He hoped desperately that, when the time arrived, he wouldn't freeze up at the prospect of lying in bed next to Elizabeth, acutely conscious that the heart beating in her body was that of the only other girl who had lain on that bed with him. He and Charlotte had never made love; although they had come pretty close at times. They both felt they were too young, despite the fact they had both passed the legal age. With Elizabeth it was different. They were older and more mature, and both felt the time was right. Elizabeth didn't want to go on the Pill, because of her medical history, so Dennis had agreed to be responsible for contraception. Tonight, they had agreed, would be the night.

At the end of the film, Dennis switched off the TV and

tidied away the pizza wrappings. He held his hand out to Elizabeth.

"You ready for bed?"

She nodded, and took his hand.

Together they went upstairs, and their relationship moved to another level.

As THEY LAY on the bed, both now unclothed, but both a little shy about proceeding, Elizabeth took Dennis's hand and placed it over her heart.

"It's beating strongly in there, Dennis. I think she would approve of us being together. She loved you, and would have wanted you to be happy, and not spend your life mourning her."

Dennis lifted his head and placed his ear on her breast. Yes, there was the steady beat of a healthy heart. He decided that, although he could never forget whose heart was beating inside Elizabeth, he would believe her words. Charlotte was a loving girl. She wouldn't have wanted him to be unhappy.

That night, it being a first for them both, their love-making was slow and tender. Their relationship was eventually fully consummated just before midnight. Afterwards, they lay in each other's arms, kissing each other from time to time, and murmuring sweet sentiments.

"That was beautiful, Dennis. It was everything I always dreamed it would be."

"You don't regret going all the way, do you?"

"No, I don't regret anything. Do you?"

"No, nothing at all…not a thing."

They drifted to sleep in each other's arms.

· · ·

LEWIS HILL & DOREEN TRENT

"I HOPE the dinner is up to the standard you expect, Lewis. I haven't cooked much since..."

Lewis reached over the table and patted Doreen's hand.

"It's wonderful, Ma'am. Believe me, I've had some god-awful...oh, excuse me, some awful meals in my life; especially in recent years. I was in an institution for a while, back home, and believe me, the meals were pretty bad."

"Thank you. That's nice of you to say. And don't worry about moderating your language on my account. I'm no fragile flower, believe me. Oh, and please call me Doreen. Ma'am makes me feel like the Queen."

Lewis laughed.

"Very well, Ma...sorry, Doreen."

Doreen passed over a cup of coffee from the pot she had just made.

"You mentioned an institution. Would it be an intrusion for me to ask you about that? You don't have to tell me if you don't want to."

"That's fine, Doreen. I don't mind telling you. I have had mental health problems on several occasions over the years; since I was in the US Army. I went a bit crazy for a while; not helped because I was drinking at the time. I was sent to an institution and received some treatment. But you need have no worries about me on that score. I gave up the drink for good a year ago."

Doreen looked at him sympathetically. She knew all about drink and its consequences.

"I had a problem too. My daughter—my only child—was

killed in a road accident, when she was just sixteen. I wanted to die. There didn't seem any point in carrying on, really. But I didn't have the guts to end it all. Instead I took to the drink. It probably would have finished me off eventually, but I met Grace Bennett, the vicar, and she helped me turn my life around. It was her suggestion that I took in a lodger."

Lewis didn't let on that he had heard her story already, but preferred to let her tell it herself. There sure was a lot of suffering in the world. Coming here, originally as some sort of revenge trip, had turned his life around. Sure, he was still torn up inside about what had happened to him, but he had learned to cope better with it. The drugs he took helped too. He felt sad, rather than bitter. Sad too that the cancer was eating away at him inside. The London doctor had promised him a bit more time—perhaps a year more—well he'd darned well make it two years if he could. And he'd make the best of that time; not waste it as he had in the past.

It hadn't been a complete waste, however. There had been a few happy years; mainly due to the birth of a beautiful daughter. Of course, being him, he had messed up the relationship with her mother, who had thrown him out of her home when their daughter, Kristen, was just a few months old. He'd never told anyone about Kristen, but now he wanted to share his secret with this sad woman, who had lost her own daughter.

"I have a daughter too; a girl called Kristen. I wasn't as good a parent to her as you obviously were to your daughter. She's twenty now. I haven't seen her for nearly two years, but we've stayed in touch."

Doreen smiled at the mention of his daughter.

"That's nice that you've stayed in touch. Were you

married to her mother?"

"No, it was a fling, and she got pregnant. We moved in together, but I was drinking a lot, and having bad dreams. She was frightened for the baby, especially when I lost my temper, and threw me out when Kristen was about six months old."

"But you've managed to stay in touch. That's quite an achievement. Most men would have walked away and lost touch with their child."

"I had some treatment after that, and managed to stop drinking for a while, and Corey, my ex-girlfriend, allowed me to come and see Kristen from time to time. She was a beautiful little girl—still is. I'm so proud of her."

He paused, lost in thought, and Doreen got up to clear the table. She was pleased Lewis had opened up to her. It somehow made her feel less alone with her own dismal thoughts. She didn't know his full story, or that he had been diagnosed with terminal cancer, but from the moment she first met him she had felt a sort of kinship – a common bond of suffering. She hoped that they would both benefit from his living at her home.

DORINDA & ARTHUR

LIFE WAS GOOD, Arthur thought, as he sat in the armchair in Dorinda's sitting room. They were watching a TV film together, and Dorinda had just brought in a cup of coffee for them both. She seemed different, somehow. The slightly reserved outer shell had melted, and she smiled much more than before. He hadn't expected to find love again at his age, but maybe this warm, satisfied feeling in his body was love. It wasn't the same type of love he had felt in his early twenties, when he and his late wife had married; but a more mature, and perhaps less heady love than he had felt back then. But it was love, nonetheless, he was sure. He wondered if Dorinda felt the same, but wasn't quite confident enough to broach the question.

If it turned out she felt the same, what for the future? Would they both want to marry? Or should they simply live together, as so many people did these days, without the shame that such an existence might once have brought when he was young. Perhaps a serious conversation should take place between them before too long. In the meantime, he would just enjoy life as it now was.

He hadn't talked much to Dennis lately, but he didn't seem to be too upset at his father spending the night with Dorinda. He seemed to have other matters on his mind lately, since he and Elizabeth were seeing each other on a regular basis now. He was quite aware that Elizabeth was sometimes spending the night with Dennis, but didn't feel he could be a hypocrite and become an old-fashioned Dad in that regard. Good luck to the pair. He just hoped his son was being responsible as far as birth control was concerned, and wondered if perhaps he should say something to Dennis about it.

The film came to an end, and Dorinda got up to take the mugs back to the kitchen.

"Are you ready to head up then?" she asked.

Arthur stood and stretched.

"Yes, I think so. I have to be away from here by eight, to

pick up some supplies, before I start work at the Ferguson's."

IT WAS ABOUT three a.m. when Dorinda's cry awoke Arthur. It was a strange mewling sound of distress. He switched on the bedside light and turned to see. What was the matter? Dorinda was still asleep, but seemed to be having a bad dream. He touched her gently to try to soothe her, and her eyes sprung open. There was an alarmed look on her face.

"What's the matter? I didn't mean it, you know. She wouldn't stop."

"You're having a bad dream, Dorinda."

He reached over and stroked her arm to calm her, but wondered what she meant when she said she wouldn't stop. Was she talking about her mother? He had never asked her to explain the events on the night her mother died, preferring to let the past remain in the past. Dorinda began to cry; large tears running down her cheeks and dripping on to the sheet below. Arthur pulled her towards him and put his arms around her.

"There, there. It's alright. You were just having a dream."

Dorinda clung to him and gradually the tears stopped. Arthur reached over and picked a tissue from the box by the bed, and handed it to her.

"Do you want to talk about it? What were you dreaming about?"

Dorinda was reluctant to talk at first, but then, in a flat, quiet voice, she told Arthur what had disturbed her.

"My mother. I told the police that I had no memory of what had happened. I didn't. I must have blanked it out, I think. They said I had killed her while the balance of my mind was disturbed. That I wasn't aware of what I had done. But it came back. My memory. I knew I'd done it. She wouldn't stop. Going on and on. I couldn't take any more. So, I hit her—hard. I wanted to shut her up forever."

Then she began to cry again. Arthur was stunned into silence. If what Dorinda had said was correct, and that she had knowingly hit her mother with the intention of shutting her up, then she would have faced a murder charge, which carried an automatic life sentence. Her barrister had somehow convinced the jury that there was nothing premeditated about her actions, and they had been sympathetic to her plight. Somehow, Arthur couldn't think of Dorinda as being a cold-blooded murderess, but in reality, that's what she was.

He looked down at the woman in his arms, his feelings disturbed. Dorinda, meanwhile, had clearly only partially woken up and dropped off to sleep again. He lay awake for a long time, emotions revolving through his brain, wondering how he would deal with this new information. Would it change what he thought about Dorinda? He didn't know.

The following morning, Arthur left early to go to work, leaving Dorinda still sleeping. He was glad they wouldn't be having a conversation over breakfast, because he was so conflicted and needed time to process what she had told him the night before.

On the drive to that day's job, he wondered if there was someone he could talk to; someone who would listen and not jump to hasty judgement; someone who would keep their conversation confidential, and not immediately report it to the police. He drove past the church and wondered if perhaps Grace Bennett, the vicar, might be someone to whom he might unburden himself. He knew that Anglican clergy, unlike their Catholic counterparts, did not normally listen to their parishioner's confessions. But, surely, she would offer wise counsel. He was aching to unburden himself.

That afternoon, on his way home, he stopped off at the church, and spotted the vicar walking through the church-yard, towards the church. He waved, and she responded; waiting for him to catch her up.

"Hello, Vicar, can you spare me a moment?"

"Yes, of course, Arthur. Would you like to come into the church while we chat? There's no one there."

He wondered if his face conveyed an anxious message, that she should agree to stop whatever she was doing to talk to him. Grace didn't bombard him with questions immedi-ately, which was a relief to Arthur. He needed time to phrase his questions. They sat down on a couple of the comfortable chairs, which had replaced the hard, wooden pews, when the church was refurbished a year earlier, and Grace smiled encouragingly.

"This is difficult, Vicar..." He paused for a moment, before continuing. "If I talk to you about someone else, will it remain confidential—between the two of us?"

"Yes, Arthur, it will. You have my word on that."

"Good. It concerns my lady friend, Dorinda Lake. You know her, don't you?"

"I do, Arthur. She comes to the church from time to time. I heard that you two were now a couple. Is she well?"

"She is, but, well, I expect you know her past, don't you?"

"I know something about her past, but I would rather not

divulge what I know. Confidentiality has to go both ways, you understand."

"Of course, Vicar. I understand completely. I won't ask you for any information, but I have learned something from her that worries me greatly."

Arthur proceeded to tell the Vicar about events the previous night.

"I'm not sure if she was fully awake when she told me that, or whether she was still dreaming. But it has set my mind racing something awful, and I don't know what to do."

The vicar remained silent for a moment, obviously assimilating the information that had just come her way. She spoke carefully and slowly; perhaps concerned in case she was unwise in her choice of words.

"That is quite a burden that has landed on your shoulders, Arthur. What are your thoughts on the subject?"

"I'll be honest, vicar; it's thrown my mind into a right turmoil. I don't know what to think."

"How would you summarise your relationship with Dorinda? I don't mean I want the details—just, what do you feel about her? Do you value her as a person? Do you have strong feelings about her nature and her character?"

"I've become very fond of her, to be honest. I never thought, after I lost my wife, that I could be happy with anyone else; but I've been happy and contented in my relationship with Dorinda. I knew what she had done; and I knew she had paid the price for it. But that was when I thought it was done while her mind was disturbed, and that it hadn't been pre-meditated. But now I'm not so sure. Don't get me wrong, Vicar. I'm not saying I'm afraid that she might do something like that again—I don't. But, could she be charged again with murder, after serving time for manslaughter? I thought people couldn't be charged twice for the same offence."

Grace looked at Arthur compassionately; understanding the anguish he seemed to be feeling.

"There used to be a rule of double jeopardy, that meant that people couldn't be charged again for a crime, if they had previously been found innocent of the same crime, even if fresh evidence had come to light. However, that ruling has now changed, and I'm afraid that people can now be charged again for the same crime. But is there any evidence that Dorinda was aware of what she was about to do?"

"Not that I know of."

"So, any future case would rest on you giving evidence about what you heard her say?"

"Yes, I suppose so. But would either of us be believed? And what good would it do now? It wouldn't bring her mother back. And Dorinda has already been punished for the lesser crime. What good would it serve, her going back to prison?"

"I can't tell you what to do, Arthur. That is between you and your conscience. I believe you need to think it through very carefully; to try to decide on the answers to the questions you've just posed. And think about what would be the consequences of either course of action; reporting her or not reporting her; what would be gained, and what lost."

Arthur seemed lost in thought, and Grace leaned forward and patted the back of his hand. She continued talking.

"If you want some legal advice, you should be able to get some, where confidentiality is guaranteed. They would be able to explain to you what would happen if you reported this information to the police. But feel free to come and talk to me at any time in the future. My door is always open."

"Thank you, vicar. I'm very grateful for you listening to me. I will give the matter some more thought."

As he walked back to his van, Arthur was reflective. He would need to ponder on what, if anything, he should do. Meanwhile, at her home, Dorinda was seeing off one of her students, and wondered why Arthur hadn't sent her his usual lunchtime text today.

CHAPTER 11

 RISTEN HILL

ON THE BUS back to her mother's apartment in Brooklyn, Kristen played with her cell phone, checking on emails and social media posts. It had been a long time since she had heard from her Dad—about six months, she thought—and wondered where he was. She hoped he hadn't started drinking again. Once again, she sent him a message, and hoped that this time she would receive a response.

As she reached home, she came upon her half-brother, Tommy, playing with his game on the stairs.

"Hiya, Tommy. Why are you sitting out here?"

She had to wait a few seconds before he could drag himself away from the screen, but eventually he looked up at his big sister.

"Hey, Kris. Mom said I was driving her mad with the noise of the game, so I came out here."

"Don't you have your ear buds?"

"Nah. Left them at school."

"Well it's Friday, so you're going to have to wait until Monday to get them. You going to sit out here until then?"

He laughed, knowing she was joshing him. They got along pretty good, considering the ten years between them and that they didn't see each other so much, now that Kristen was at college.

She left him on the stairs, immersed in another game, and went into the apartment, rather hoping that Vincent, her mother's partner, and Tommy's father, wouldn't be home. He was okay, but she found him a bit boring, and usually monopolised the conversation. It would be nice to have a one-on-one chat with her Mom for a change. She only came home about once a month these days, with so much else going on in her life right now. Exams weren't that far away, and she was also busy with her part-time job.

"Hi Mom."

She heard her Mom's response from the kitchen, and went in to find her sitting at the breakfast bar, reading the paper and drinking a cup of coffee.

"Hi honey. You okay? I didn't realise how the time was going on. Thought I would have a few minutes with the paper before I start on dinner."

"You stay there. I can make a start if you like? What are we having?"

"Thanks, Kris. That's sweet of you. I have some lamb chops in the fridge, and plenty of root vegetables. I thought I would make a hearty stew to try and fill that little brother of yours. I swear, I don't know where he puts all the food he eats. But pour yourself a coffee first. It's freshly made."

Kristen sat opposite her mother and began peeling vegetables – a mug of hot coffee at her side. She was glad that Vincent wasn't yet home. It was rare that she and her mother were alone these days. Corey looked up from the newspaper, aware her daughter was watching her.

"You okay, honey. Everything alright at school?"

"Yes, Mom, everything's fine. I'm worried about my Dad though. I haven't heard from him in months. I've sent some texts, but had no reply."

Corey reached over the breakfast bar and touched her daughter's hand.

"I'm sure he will be okay, Kris. He may be back on the drink, sadly. I'm sure he will surface again before too long."

"Yes, I guess he will."

Kristen continued the slow, rhythmic peeling of the carrots and parsnips for the stew, lost in thought. She wanted to talk about Lewis, but was afraid to in case Vincent or Tommy walked in. Vincent, in particular, became irritated if Lewis' name ever came up in conversation. He probably wished her Dad would disappear for good, Kristen thought.

Corey sensed her daughter wanted to talk.

"Tell me," she asked. "I know something's bothering you."

Kristen paused her peeling.

"It's not bothering me. But I've been thinking about him more, that's all. I've just had a gut feeling that something is wrong. That's why I tried to contact him. I think of him being all alone—no family—and I want to reach out to him. Maybe I can help him."

"I don't think you can, Kris. Your Dad has a lot of problems. Drink is only one of them. They date back a long way. Long before you were born. I tried to help him; I really did. But he wouldn't let me. In the end I had to take us both away from him for our safety. He became aggressive at times, when he was drunk; and I wasn't prepared to let him harm you."

Kristen didn't respond to her mother's claim that her father might have hurt her. She was certain that he wouldn't harm a hair on her head. From her childhood memories, she had never known a time when her father's anger had been directed at her.

Her phone rang, and both women jumped, as the noise punctured the silence. Kristen picked it up and saw a number she didn't recognize.

"Hello," she began, cautiously. The familiar sound of her Dad's voice came into her ear.

"Hi, Kris. You sounded startled. Did I make you jump?"

"Just a little, Dad. I'm at Mom's, and we were just talking about you when you rang."

"Oh dear, that sounds ominous. Say hi to your Mom for me."

"Dad says hi," she whispered to her mother, before continuing the conversation with her Dad.

"I've been worried about you. I've sent several texts and heard nothing back from you."

"Unfortunately, I lost my phone. Had to get a new one. Life was a little chaotic for a while, but it's better now."

"Oh Dad. I thought you were going to try and leave chaos behind, last time we talked. Where are you?"

"You might be surprised, but I'm in England."

"England, wow. What are you doing there?"

"It's a long story—bit complicated. I was sick for a while, but I'm getting better," he lied.

Corey reached over and took the board with the chopped vegetables away from Kristen and continued with the supper preparations, allowing her daughter to concentrate on the call.

"I'm glad to hear that, Dad. Where are you? London?"

"No, I'm in a small town in Oxfordshire. It's not too far from London. A friend of mine found me a nice place to stay. I thought I would stick around here for a while. I don't suppose there's any chance you could get over to see me, is there? I'd love to see you again. It's been such a long time."

Kristen detected a wistfulness in his voice, and wondered if her father was being entirely honest with her.

"I'd love to see you too. I guess it might be possible. The semester ends in two weeks. I guess I could perhaps fly over for a few days. I'll talk it over with Mom and get back to you. Give me your details. Hang on, let me get a pen."

She grabbed a pen and paper from the breakfast bar and jotted down her Dad's address.

"I'll call you back tomorrow, shall I?"

"Okay, honey. Bye then. Love to your Mom and Tommy."

So it was that two weeks later, Kristen stepped through the Arrivals door at Heathrow Airport, anxiously looking around for her Dad's face. There he was, standing next to an unknown man. He looked thinner than when she had last seen him, and a little pale, but had the same big grin on his face. He shouted and waved his arm.

"Hi honey. Here we are."

He gave her a bear hug, as big as if he hadn't seen her in in a decade, before pulling back to look her in her face.

"Kris, you don't know how good it is to see you. You look as pretty as ever."

He turned towards the man standing next to her.

"This is an old army buddy, Mac—sorry, it's Grant now. Mac, this is my daughter, Kristen."

"Hi Grant. Or do you prefer Mac?"

Grant gave her a grin, and shook her hand.

"I don't mind. But probably better to go with Grant. Anyone who knows me now wouldn't know who you were talking to if you said Mac. I think your Dad finds it hard to make the change. But I make allowances for him."

The three headed for the car park, Grant pulling Kristen's suitcase, allowing Lewis to put his arm around his daughter's shoulder. The conversation on the journey back to Swinbury was light and free-flowing, of the catch-up variety. Lewis wanted to know what she had been doing, and how was her Mom, and Kristen's plans for the future. He gave her very little opportunity to question him. But Kristen was tired, anyway, and was happy to leave more in-depth questions until the following day.

Grant joined in the conversation as they neared home.

"Where your Dad is lodging, there's no spare room, so my partner, Jennifer, and I, thought you could stay with us while you're here, and one of us would be more than happy to take you over to see your Dad at any time. Plus, of course, he can come to us at any time. I hope that suits you?"

Kristen was happy with the arrangements, and looked forward to getting some sleep above anything. The last day or two had been hectic, arranging everything to come over here, plus the flight. If her Dad was happy with the arrangements, then so was she.

As they dropped Lewis off at Doreen's house, Lewis gave his daughter another big hug, while Grant rang the bell for Doreen, who appeared within seconds. He turned back to Lewis and Kristen.

"Hey, you two, I suggest we give Kristen the morning to sleep in tomorrow, Lewis. How about I pick you up at around three p.m., and you can stay to dinner. I'll bring you back here in the evening."

The arrangement seemed to suit everyone, including Doreen, who wanted to know Lewis's meal arrangements while his daughter was here, and they parted company until the following day.

On the short drive back to Jennifer and Grant's home, Grant kept the conversation light. He knew from Lewis that Kristen had no idea how ill her father was. It wasn't for him to pass on any secrets. That was between Lewis and his daughter. But he was glad she had come. There were days when Lewis didn't look as though he would make the predicted year of life, let alone the two years that Lewis himself was hoping for. He would do anything to ensure that his former colleague was happy during this difficult time. The two had now come to an understanding of the past, and forgiveness on the part of Lewis, for something he now acknowledged wasn't Grant's fault.

As they arrived home, Grant introduced Kristen to Jennifer, and showed her where she was sleeping—a charming bedroom, overlooking the garden at the back, that Jennifer, with her home-making skills, had made pretty and inviting, for this, their first guest.

. . .

LEWIS HILL & KRISTEN HILL

JENNIFER AND KRISTEN hit it off immediately, despite the difference in ages. Kristen was fascinated to hear Jennifer talk about all the places in the world she had visited as part of her job as a newspaper reporter.

"You've had some exciting trips—awesome really. That's something I would love to do when I've finished studying."

"Yes, I thoroughly enjoyed it. But it has changed so much since I first started. The advent of social media has begun to make newspaper reporting somewhat redundant. Unless they go online, they will be lucky to survive."

"That's a shame; but I understand what you're saying. My generation don't read newspapers in the way that yours did. But I must admit, I do enjoy sitting down on a Sunday afternoon at my Mom's, and having a good read of the paper. I just don't have time in the week."

Jennifer made a pot of coffee when the two men arrived, and enjoyed light conversation while it was drunk. Grant then jumped up.

"Okay, you guys; Kristen has come all this way to see her Dad, and you and I, Jennifer, have books to write, so why don't we make ourselves scarce and leave you two to catch up. You can either stay here; or if you want some fresh air, there's a small park not too far from here where you can have a stroll. We thought we would have dinner about seven, if that's okay with you?"

Soon the two hosts had vanished, and Kristen came to sit next to her father on the sofa.

"I'm so pleased to see you again, Dad. Although I'm a bit concerned about you losing weight since I last saw you."

Lewis took her hand.

"Yeah, well, I haven't exactly looked after myself in recent years, as you well know. When I came here, I was in a mess, but Mac took care of me. Believe me, I'm a lot better than I was. I'll tell you all about it in a while. But first, I want to find out more about you."

They chatted, and soon an hour had passed. Lewis stood up and looked out of the window, where the sun kept peeking out from behind some clouds.

"Looks good out there. How about we go for a walk, as Mac suggested?"

Kristen seemed keen, and a few minutes later they were strolling down the road, arm in arm, towards the park. Once there, they sat on a bench, next to a small lake, where a group of ducks were swimming lazily around. Having ascertained that the visitors had not brought bread for them, they soon swam away.

Lewis patted the slats of the bench.

"I've slept on one or two benches like this in my time, believe me. I've not exactly been a role model for you, have I, honey? I let the drink control my life for a long time. Plus, of course, I had some mental health problems, as you might remember from when you were growing up. I've not been a great Dad to you."

Kristen squeezed his hand, and her large brown eyes welled up.

"I don't blame you for that, Dad. I know a little about

your problems. Mom told me a few things over the years. You had a tough time in the army, I believe. But there's treatment for it now, isn't there?"

"Yes, they are a lot more understanding about the problems soldiers face when they re-enter civilian life now, and I've had some help in recent years. Trouble is, I keep slipping backwards from time to time. But I think I've got the drink problem licked now."

"I'm so glad, Dad. Now we need to feed you up and get you fully better."

Lewis gave a sad smile. He wondered if now was the time to tell his daughter about his cancer, and decided to wait awhile. Let them enjoy some time together first. He didn't want the misery he had endured in the past to blight this short time with Kristen. He knew his story was being included by Mac in his autobiography, currently being written, and that his daughter would one day know the whole truth, but for now he didn't want to blight her visit. He was acutely aware that the time they had together was running out, like the sand in a giant hourglass, slipping inexorably from one globe into the other. He wanted this visit to be full of joy and help them both to store happy memories for the time ahead.

That night, dinner was a fun affair. Happy times from the past were remembered and humorous anecdotes were passed back and forth. Kristen thought how well Jennifer and Grant seemed to match, and was surprised to learn that they had only got together recently.

"Ah, but we had the excitement of a long-running affair over many years. It was just that life kept intervening in keeping us apart. But we've rectified that. I've no intention of leaving here and going back to my bachelor days—assuming that Jenny will allow me, of course."

Jennifer laughed, and looked at him fondly.

"It doesn't matter when it began; just that it doesn't end. And I've no plan to let him slip through my fingers again. He's trapped in my web now for sure."

"Darling, I couldn't think of anywhere I would rather be trapped."

Kristen laughed, and Lewis made a mock scoffing noise.

"Listen to this pair, Kristen. Like a couple of teenage lovebirds."

THE WEEK SLIPPED PAST FAR TOO QUICKLY for all of them. Grant and Jennifer took time off from their writing, to take the father and daughter to see local attractions and the beautiful countryside around them, making sure to give Lewis and Kristen as much space and privacy as possible to build up memories for the painful times they knew were ahead.

At the end of the week, the two men took Kristen by car back to Heathrow, for her flight back to New York. Grant dropped them off and went to park the car; giving them a last chance for some private words. Kristen leaned into her father's chest and he enclosed her body with what had once been strong, muscular arms.

"Thank you for coming, Kris. It has meant the world to me. I know I've said it before, but I'll say it again, you are the best thing I ever did with my life. I'm so proud of the young woman you've become, and so grateful to your Mom for bringing you up so well."

Kristen was becoming tearful, so was grateful when

Grant turned up with the suitcase, and they went to the desk for Kristen to check-in. In no time they were on the way towards airport security, beyond which the two men could no longer accompany her. With a hug for Grant, she whispered to him.

"Thank you for looking after Dad. I appreciate it so much."

Grant gave her hand a squeeze, and diplomatically turned away while Lewis said goodbye to his daughter.

"Bye Dad. I love you. I'll text you when I reach New York. In the meantime, you take care of yourself, and do everything the doctor tells you."

"I love you, Kris. More than you'll ever know. Safe travels."

He turned away, so his daughter did not see the tears beginning to trickle down his cheeks. But she too had wet cheeks. With a last wave, she went through the entrance to the security area, and was soon out of sight.

Grant patted his friend on the shoulder. Words seemed inadequate right now; and the two men turned for the journey home, with unspoken words hanging in the air. The return home was a quiet affair.

CHAPTER 12

ARTHUR & DORINDA

SINCE HIS DISCUSSION with the vicar over Dorinda's night-time "confession", Arthur hadn't mentioned the event, but Dorinda knew that something was different. One evening, she decided to confront him.

"Is there something wrong, Arthur? You seem a little distant these days."

"No…no, nothing wrong."

But he paused, and clearly looked as though he had something more to say. Dorinda waited.

"Actually, I have had something on my mind. Perhaps we should talk about it."

He told her of the night of Dorinda's bad dream,

repeating word for word what she had said. Dorinda looked horrified. She had clearly not remembered any of it.

"I said all that. Why didn't you tell me the next day, Arthur? Did I upset you in what I said?"

He reached over and patted her hand.

"It made me think, I suppose, rather than upset me. You realise the implications of what you said, do you?"

He didn't spell them out, but Dorinda was an intelligent woman, and didn't need him to explain.

"Yes. It means that my killing mother was premeditated. That I should have been convicted of murder, and not manslaughter. I suppose that has occurred to you too, Arthur?"

"Yes, it did. I've been thinking about it a lot."

Dorinda's face looked anxious. She had come to trust Arthur, and depend on him emotionally. Was all this going to change things between them?

"And what was the result of all the thought?"

Arthur tried to calm her obvious anxiety.

"Don't be afraid. I'm not about to march to the police station and demand they re-arrest you. I didn't talk to you straight away. I needed time to think about things."

"And what conclusions did you reach?"

"I actually—and don't be angry at this—I spoke to someone and asked for advice. I'd rather not say who at this point; and they calmed some of my fears. On the other hand, the law of double jeopardy has changed, and it is possible that you could be charged again with murder."

Dorinda gasped a little, and pulled her hand away from his. But Arthur grabbed it back.

"I'm on your side, Dorinda, remember that. I will only do

something that won't harm you. There is no way that I want your past to be dug up again. This person who advised me suggested we get some legal advice."

Tears began to roll down Dorinda's cheeks as her past, that she had tried to forget, came to the surface once again.

"I can't go back to prison again, Arthur. It would mean ten or more years. I couldn't bear it. My life would be over."

Arthur was devastated by her reaction, and wished he had never raised the subject. He should have simply forgotten what she had said. But it would be more difficult now to bury the past, with doubts and fears hanging over them. He stood up and went to her side, pulling her body into his, and caressing her hair.

"You won't go back to prison, Dorinda. I'm determined about that. I know you are a good, kind woman, who was goaded past her own endurance level. Don't distress yourself. We'll work this out."

They remained clinging to each other, in silence, for some time. Finally, Dorinda broke the silence.

"Whatever happens, Arthur, there is no way I want to drag you into this; for you to become an accomplice after the fact. I think we should seek legal advice, as your confidant suggested. I'm sure that anything we say to them would be confidential."

Arthur was relieved that Dorinda had come to this decision by herself, without any pressure from him.

TWO WEEKS LATER, they found themselves in the office of a solicitor in a nearby town. They both preferred a stranger, rather than someone they might bump into on the High

Street of Swinbury. Joshua Reynolds was a middle-aged, kindly-looking man, who welcomed them into his office and listened quietly while they both told their stories. At the end, he stroked his chin in thought.

"Interesting story; and I appreciate your disquiet. Firstly, I need to check; are you two living together as husband or wife, or civil partners?"

Arthur answered for them both.

"No. We are partners who sometimes cohabit; but we have no formal relationship."

"If you were married or in a civil partnership, then it is unlikely, Arthur, that you would be asked to testify against Dorinda. There are certain circumstances when you may be compelled, but yours do not come under this heading. However, as an independent person, then it is possible that you could be compelled to testify on behalf of any prosecution case against Dorinda."

He paused, while both his clients digested his statement. He continued.

"I take it that there is no other evidence that might back up what you said as you were waking from a bad dream? It would simply be the word of Arthur?"

Dorinda replied, this time, in a quiet, nervous voice.

"No. At least, I don't think so. I had buried the event so deep in my memory, that I had convinced myself that what I did to my mother happened without premeditation, and that it was a mental aberration. Now, I'm not sure if that's the truth."

"I can't tell you what decisions, if any, you should take, Dorinda. But on the basis of what I have heard today I can state a few facts. Firstly, a court of law has already tried you for both murder and manslaughter, and your barrister seems to have convinced the jury, without too much trouble, that the murder charge should be thrown out. You only served a short sentence because of that. I think the same barrister should be able to dismiss any repeated charge of murder, if you pleaded 'Not Guilty'. If Arthur was forced to give evidence, that might sway them a little, but I'm sure the barrister would be able to sow sufficient doubt in the jury's mind to allow a 'Not Guilty' result. If Arthur was in a permanent relationship with you, it is unlikely that he would even be called to give evidence."

He turned to Arthur.

"If you are concerned, Arthur, about the possibility of being charged with accessory after the fact, then as with Dorinda, it would simply be one word against another. In my opinion, it is unlikely that such an event would occur."

He then turned to Dorinda.

"Murder is a very serious offence, as you know, Dorinda. But I have heard enough and seen enough to be sure in my own mind that you were properly convicted of manslaughter, rather than murder. You served your time and were properly punished under the Law. But I don't feel any good would be served in seeking further punishment. By all means seek therapy if you feel it is necessary. But my advice to you both is to forget that night and continue to live your lives without fear."

As they left the solicitor's office, Arthur took Dorinda's hand, and felt happier than he had for a while. He had a plan formulating in his mind.

·   ·   ·

TWO DAYS LATER, Arthur turned up at the usual time at Dorinda's, looking smarter than usual, wearing a jacket and tie.

"You look very smart tonight, Arthur. Is this a special occasion?"

"I thought I would take you out for dinner, Dorinda. We haven't exactly been on a proper date, have we? I thought it was time we did. Pop and change, if you want to. I have a table booked at that Italian restaurant in town."

Forty minutes later they arrived at the restaurant, holding hands, as they did more frequently now. They were shown to a secluded table in the corner, that Arthur had requested, and a bottle of wine was opened. He was unusually nervous tonight. He raised his glass and clinked it with Dorinda's.

"Here's to us."

He put down his glass on the table and reached into his pocket, to make sure the little box was still there. He took Dorinda's hand in his.

"Dorinda, I've discovered a new lease of life since we met. Being with you makes me very happy and contented. In fact, I am in love with you. Will you do me the honour of marrying me?"

Dorinda gasped as Arthur drew a ring box from his pocket and took out a diamond engagement ring. She was lost for words. For the first time in her life, someone had said they loved her. In fact, she was quite overwhelmed, and unable to speak at first; but a joyful tear trickled down her cheek. Arthur smiled.

"I hope your lack of words is a good sign."

"Yes, yes...of course, yes."

Her voice came back to her.

"Arthur, you don't know how touched I am to hear you say that. I love you too. I would be honoured to be your wife."

They both beamed at each other like teenage lovebirds as Arthur placed the ring on Dorinda's finger.

A flicker of anxiety crossed her face.

"It's not just because of...you know, what we discussed at the solicitor's office the other day?"

"Well that might have speeded up my thinking; but, no, my love is genuine. I'm a bit old-fashioned, and I didn't think the vicar would approve of us living in sin, so to speak. But the bonus is that when we are married, I cannot be compelled to testify against you. So that is an added advantage."

The food arrived, delivered by a grinning waiter, who had spotted the open ring box on the table. They had young couples proposing in the restaurant before, but it was nice to see a mature couple so obviously in love.

THEY WANTED A QUIET WEDDING, to take place sooner rather than later, but Dorinda was keen for a church wedding, rather than in the Registry Office. They went to see Grace Bennett, who was delighted to hear their news.

"I'm thrilled for you both. This is wonderful news."

Of course, she wasn't party to the reason why they wanted to marry quickly, but told them they would have to wait the requisite three weeks, while the Banns were read. The date was fixed. Grace hoped that none of her parishioners raised objections to a convicted killer being married in church. She decided that perhaps, next Sunday, when she called the Banns for the first time, she would make forgiveness the subject of her weekly sermon.

"WHO SHALL WE INVITE?" whispered Dorinda, as they lay cuddling in bed that night.

"I thought Dennis and Elizabeth, as our two official witnesses, if that's alright with you?"

"Yes, of course. I thought I might invite Doreen Trent; the woman who lost her daughter in a traffic accident. I have become quite friendly with her through the church. And she has a nice American man friend now, who lodges with her, and sometimes comes to church with her. I think they are just friends though."

Arthur made his suggestion next.

"That sounds good. How about Lewis's friend, Grant, and his partner, Jennifer? They've not been in the town very long, but I remember Jennifer from when we were children. She had a twin sister, Juliet, who drowned in the river when she was just four. It was so sad. I bumped into them both in the supermarket a couple of weeks ago, and we had a long chat. They seem a lovely couple."

"Yes, I've chatted to Jennifer on a few occasions. She's a charming woman. She tells me she's writing a novel at the moment. Used to be a journalist, didn't she?"

"That's right. She's so interesting to talk to. I think that will be enough, don't you? We can book the small room at the golf club for a reception afterwards. How does that idea sound?"

"It sounds perfect."

They kissed goodnight, and drifted off to sleep.

THE BANNS WERE READ SATISFACTORILY for the first Sunday, with no objections heard. It was the second Sunday that proved troublesome. Grace Bennett read the Banns from the pulpit, after her sermon, as was her custom. She barely paused after reading the two names of Arthur and Dorinda, expecting no objections as the previous Sunday. But the second she read the second name, Dorinda Trent, when a woman near the back of the church stood up and shouted "No."

Grace stopped talking, unsure at first from whom the objection was coming. A small woman, in her sixties she thought, stepped out into the aisle and called out loudly and clearly.

"That woman is a murderer; and you are allowing her to marry in this church? Shame on you."

Grace was temporarily lost for words, but managed to eventually get some words out. The woman, Cecily McDonald, was known to her. She was renowned for being plain-speaking and strong willed.

"Mrs McDonald, would you like to come forward please. There's no need to stand at the back and shout. Please come to the front."

The woman walked to the front of the church; her mouth set in a straight, firm line. Grace tried to lower the temperature and, when she drew near, lowered her voice so that only Mrs McDonald could hear what she said.

"I understand your objections, Mrs McDonald. Can we discuss the matter after the service is over please?"

Grace was unsure what the etiquette for such an intervention was; it had never happened to her before, so she simply used her own judgement. Cecily McDonald glared at her, but also dropped the volume of her voice.

"I think it should be discussed in front of the whole congregation. The Banns were addressed to us all. There may be others who share my views."

In the meantime, Arthur and Dorinda sat in their seats in the third row of the pews, feeling and looking stunned. It hadn't occurred to either of them that someone would stand up in church and make an objection like this. They watched helplessly as the vicar and the objector engaged in conversation out of earshot.

Eventually, the vicar returned to the pulpit, and Mrs McDonald sat down on the first row of the pews, her arms clasped across her chest, and her body stiffly upright. The vicar once again addressed the congregation.

"I'm sorry to delay you all, but as I have received an objection to the Banns being called, I feel there is no alternative but to turn to the whole congregation. The two people in question are in the church, but I don't wish to point them out. Some of you will know them. Some will not. But I won't make this into a witch-hunt. The facts of the matter are indisputable. One of the pair was convicted of the offence of manslaughter, for the death of a family member. She was judged to have committed this offence while the balance of her mind was disturbed, and sentenced to three years in prison. Since coming out, the woman has been a model citizen, and has fallen in love with a local man, and they decided they wanted to marry. Last Sunday, those who were here will remember that I preached about forgiveness, and how God, in His mercy, forgives the sinner who has truly repented of his sin. I am satisfied that the person in question has repented and should be forgiven. This lady, Mrs McDonald, is entitled to her view and entitled to raise an objection. I would like to see if others share her view. Would you kindly raise your hand if you feel that this marriage service should not be conducted in the church?"

There was silence for several seconds, before one hand was raised; followed by another, until six hands were raised. Grace made a mental note of who the six people were.

"Thank you for your views. I don't intend to make a decision about whether the marriage should go ahead. I need to consult the Bishop, and our decision will be announced in church next Sunday. Now, if we can sing the final hymn."

Mrs Mc Donald stomped back to her pew at the back, satisfied that her complaint had at least been listened to. She didn't personally know the couple concerned; although almost everyone in the town knew their names, and she had no idea when walking past the third row of pews, that the couple in question were staring at her as she passed. She was just doing her duty as a Christian member of the church, she told herself.

As they left the church, dismay showing on their faces at being the centre of dissent during the service, there were many who looked sympathetically at them. But a few whispered to others behind the backs of their hands, and Dorinda in particular, wanted to get away from the church as soon as possible.

No sooner had they arrived back at Dorinda's home, than she burst into tears. Arthur attempted to console her.

"There, there, Dorinda. Don't feel too sad. There were

just a handful of the congregation supported that woman. Most of them seemed very understanding. Let's hope it's all sorted by next Sunday, and we can go ahead with the wedding as planned."

He put his arms around her and held her while the tears flowed, and then stopped.

"There we are. Over now. Don't upset yourself. We are bound to meet a few people like that in the future. We just have to ignore them. If the church won't marry us, then we will simply have a Registry Office ceremony. The main thing is, that I am marrying you no matter who objects."

Dorinda smiled through her tears.

"Oh Arthur, you are such a good man. I'm so lucky to have you in my life."

THE FOLLOWING DAY, they received a telephone call from the vicar.

"I'm sorry about what happened yesterday. I hope it hasn't caused you too much distress. I have spoken to the Bishop today, and we have decided that your wedding should continue, despite the objection raised. I will speak to Mrs McDonald and explain this to her, and that she must accept it. The church supports you, as do most of the congregation, it seems. If she continues to object, then, regretfully, I will have to ask her to stay away from the church, and find somewhere else to worship. Hopefully, she will drop her objection."

After the end of the call, Dorinda and Arthur discussed the wedding, now only two weeks away.

"What will we do if she turns up on the day, and makes a

fuss? Do you think we should call off the church wedding and marry in the Registry Office?"

Arthur was firm in his reply.

"No, I do not. I want to marry you in church, whatever that woman says. Don't worry, my dear, I'm sure it will be fine on the day."

The wedding was booked for Wednesday at twelve noon. At eleven thirty, he and Dennis arrived at the church, while Elizabeth and Dorinda waited at home, for the car that was to take them both to the church. Already at the church were the handful of guests; Grant and Jennifer, smartly dressed for a wedding for which they had initially been surprised to have been invited. Accompanying them were Lewis and Doreen; Lewis looking pale, and leaning heavily on Doreen. They went straight into the church, so Lewis could sit down. Grant and Jennifer were about to follow them in, when they saw Mrs McDonald marching along the path towards the church, carrying a saucepan and spoon. She was clearly intent on making a scene. She wasn't alone, either. Walking behind her, looking a little embarrassed, was a reporter from the local newspaper. He had been told by the Editor to attend in case a fracas ensued, but his sympathies were probably more with the couple about to be wed.

Arthur and Dennis had already entered the church by the time Mrs McDonald arrived, and the bride and Elizabeth were due to arrive within minutes. Grant whispered a few words to Jennifer, and walked towards the woman, who had already started banging her saucepan with the spoon, and calling out "Murderer."

"Mrs McDonald. Can I have a word with you please?"

She stopped banging and glared at him.

155

"I'm here to right a wrong. A murderer should not be allowed to marry in a Christian church."

In the meantime, Jennifer had engaged the reporter in a conversation, and drew him into the church porch, so he couldn't hear the conversation between Grant and Mrs McDonald.

Grant did his best to look intense and a little belligerent, in his best army stance. He had dealt with many fierce terrorists in his time, but actually this fierce English woman looked like she could take him on any day. Nevertheless, he had to attempt to quieten her down.

"You may think you have right on your side, Ma'am, but let me tell you that you are breaking the law."

He had no idea if she was, but it didn't hurt to make the accusation.

"This is private property, and you are breaching the peace. The question is, do you want to stop your foolish protest and leave, or do you want to wait for the police to arrive, and have your arrest witnessed by the local reporter? It won't look good on the front page of the newspaper, will it?"

Mrs McDonald stopped banging on the pan and ceased to shout. In fact, her face looked decidedly anxious. Grant's words clearly had her rattled. Her words of protest became much quieter.

"But it shouldn't be allowed. She's a murderer and shouldn't be allowed to marry in a church."

"Ma'am, the vicar has the express consent of the Bishop. Dorinda was, in fact, found guilty of manslaughter, and not murder, and there is a big difference. She has paid her debt to society and is entitled to the forgiveness of God, the same as anyone else." Just to reinforce his words, he bent closer to the woman, his face just inches from hers, and growled at her. "So, I suggest you cease this protest before the police arrive."

He drew his phone from his pocket, and began to press the numbers. Mrs McDonald looked suitably intimidated and began to back away, before turning and marching down the church path, muttering to herself. Grant smiled, and hoped he hadn't overdone the intimidation. He walked back to the porch, where the reporter was suitably impressed by some of the stories he was hearing from this former foreign correspondent.

"I think the protesting lady has changed her mind."

At that moment, the car bearing Dorinda and Elizabeth, drew up at the church gate. Everyone breathed a sigh of relief that the crisis had been averted. The reporter said goodbye, and Grant and Jennifer went into the church, to take their places. Dorinda had opted not to have anyone give her away, so she walked down the aisle, wearing a pretty, floral, summer dress, and carrying a posy of flowers, followed by Elizabeth. Arthur turned to watch her walk towards him, and grinned with pride.

The service was short and sweet. The pair had opted to have no hymns, but suitable music was played over the speakers at various points. The vicar gave her blessing and pronounced them as man and wife. All was complete in twenty minutes—probably the quickest marriage ceremony Grace had conducted in her time in the church. She was invited to join them for lunch at the golf club, but had to decline because of another engagement.

As they drove to the gold club, Jennifer praised Grant for his diplomatic skills.

"Whatever you said to that woman, it certainly worked."

"Well I did rather turn up the heat a little. I just hoped she didn't call my bluff and wait for the police to arrive. I might have been in hot water then."

"You did wonderfully."

"It's a pretty little church, isn't it? Perhaps we should go back for another wedding at some future point?"

Jennifer's head swivelled towards him.

"Is that, by chance, a hint of a marriage proposal?"

Grant laughed.

"Just putting you on notice, that's all."

CHAPTER 13

*L*EWIS HILL & DOREEN TRENT

LEWIS WAS FADING FAST, and he knew it. So did his friends, Grant and Jennifer. Grant wanted him to send for Kristen, but Lewis was adamant that he didn't want that.

"If I go before she comes back again, then let her remember me as she last saw me. Not this broken-down wreck of a man."

Grant didn't press the matter, and he and Jennifer, as well as Lewis's landlady, and friend, Doreen Trent, kept a close watch on him, and helped him as much as they were able. Grant tried to find out, tactfully, what Lewis wished to happen at the end.

"Can we hire a nurse for you, when you think it is time;

or do you wish to have hospice care? Your needs may be more than Doreen, Jennifer or I, are capable of offering."

"I would prefer to stay where I am, if that is okay with Doreen. She's been wonderful to me, but I wouldn't want to put too great a burden on her. Perhaps I should ask her?"

"I'm sure she wouldn't object to you staying there; and I can also arrange for a nurse to come in daily for pain medication and suchlike. I will talk to her, Lewis. No need for you to be concerned. We will take care of everything."

"Thank you, Mac. You two have been great. Also, I know you want to ask me, but don't like to, so I will say it first. When I go, I would like a service in that great little church where the wedding was held. Doreen and I have been going fairly often in recent months, and I have a soft spot for the vicar. Let Kristen know in good time, so she can fly over. Then I would like to be cremated, and for Kristen to take my ashes back to the States. She will know what to do with them. I'm grateful for the kindness I've found over here in England, but I'm a Yank to my bones, you know that. I want to go home."

Grant simply nodded his head and patted Lewis gently on the shoulder. It was going to be a tough time for them all, but he was determined to be there to the end for this man, with whom he once served. Although Lewis had told him, several times, he bore him no malice now about the Yemen episode, Grant knew he would feel some survivor's guilt about this to the end of his days.

DOREEN TRIED TO COOK TASTY, easily digestible food for Lewis, but he was eating less and less. The cancer nurse began to call regularly, and gave him liquid nutrition, when he could tolerate it, as well as pain killers for the pain that was often written on his face. Lewis was still able to joke to her about it.

"Well look at it this way, you have much less cooking to do now, and your food bills will be smaller."

Doreen knew he was joking, but it pained her to see him like this. She had come to like her lodger very much. Having him in the house had rescued her from the slow downward spiral she had entered after Charlotte's death. She wished she had met Lewis much sooner, and got to know him better. Her one brush with marriage to Charlotte's father had been a huge disappointment to her, and meeting Lewis reminded her that there were some good, kind men in the world, and that they weren't all callous brutes like her ex-husband.

In the evenings, when he felt up to it, they would talk, and Lewis would tell her about his life growing up in the US, and about his years in the army.

"I had a good childhood. My parents had a farm up in the Hudson Valley, north of New York, and I told Kristen a couple of years ago that I wanted her to spread my ashes up there—not in noisy Chicago, where I spent my adult years, when I wasn't travelling the world. It's kinda pretty up there, where I attended my first school, and climbed the large oak tree back of the house. Yes, I will be happy to end my time there."

When he saw Doreen's face cloud over at the mention of his ashes being scattered, he patted her hand gently.

"Don't be sad when I'm gone, Doreen. I wish we had met sooner, but I'm grateful for the time I've had with you. I hope my being here has taken a little of the pain away about your daughter. You need to get back out there and live the rest of your life as a tribute to Charlotte. You know she would have wanted it, and I know I want you to enjoy life again, even if I'm not here to see it. Promise me you won't go back to drinking, won't you?"

Doreen nodded; tears pricking her eyelids as she did so.

DENNIS & ELIZABETH

As THEY RETURNED to Dennis's home, after the wedding of his Dad and Dorinda, Dennis was quieter than usual.

"Are you okay?"

Elizabeth rested her hand on his thigh, as he was driving. He nodded.

"You're not upset at your Dad marrying again—you know, because of your Mum?"

He took one hand off the wheel as they stopped at the traffic lights and stroked her hand with his fingers.

"No, not at all. Mum would have wanted him to be happy. I was a bit surprised at the speed of it all, and disturbed by that woman shouting at the church, but not upset at him for choosing not to be lonely in his old age. After all, I won't be at home with him for ever."

The car moved forwards and he replaced his hand on the steering wheel. He had been thinking about his own future, and hoped very much that it would be with Elizabeth. Seeing Lewis at the wedding had reminded him that life was short—as if he needed to be reminded of that, after Charlotte's death at sixteen. Was it too soon to talk to Elizabeth about their future together?

He had spoken to his father a few days earlier about his plans.

"Dorinda and I will live at her house, and I want you and Elizabeth to have ours. Not that I'm pushing you into anything; but just saying, for when the time comes."

Dennis was grateful for his father's generosity. Providing a home for a future wife and family was often a struggle for people his own age, and having a house would be a huge step forward for them. But would Elizabeth want to settle down so soon, and give up any plans she might have made? She had passed her exams easily, after the extra coaching from Dorinda, and was now talking about going to college. Her dream was to work with young children; maybe a kindergarten teacher or in a nursery.

He told Elizabeth about his father's generosity, but didn't add anything about their own future. Neither did Elizabeth. They were both lost in thought as they arrived home. She was now in the habit of spending a couple of nights a week staying over with Dennis, and had originally been concerned about upsetting her father. But he hadn't seemed to mind; mindful of the difficult years she had had with her illness. He wanted whatever made her happy.

"I was sad to see Lewis today. He looked so ill."

"Yes, me too. But he was quite cheerful over lunch, even though he didn't eat anything."

Elizabeth looked up at Dennis, as they lay in bed, talking about the events of the day.

"Dennis—going through what I went through as a child

and even now, after the transplant, made me not want to waste time in my life."

"That's understandable."

"I'd rather go through life like a fast, beautiful, streak of bright light—living for the moment; not looking forwards or backwards—than just sitting waiting to die. I lived with the thought I might die for so long—and I still might, if my body begins to reject the transplants—that I want to pack as much life into the present, and not wait to do things. People just expect they are going to live for a long, long time; maybe even as long as one hundred years; but I don't think I will."

Dennis looked at her a little nervously. Was she trying to tell him something? Was something wrong of which he was unaware? She saw the fear in his eyes.

"Don't worry, Dennis. Everything is fine, as far as I know. But nothing is certain; especially for people born with life-limiting illnesses; I just don't want to wait to do things."

Dennis breathed a sigh of relief.

"I'm relieved to know there's nothing wrong. But I know what you are trying to say. What sort of things do you want to do, that you don't want to delay?"

"I don't know what your reaction will be, after such a short time together, but I want to marry you. I love you, and I want to become your wife."

Dennis smiled broadly.

"Well that's a relief. I thought you were going to say something like hand-gliding or parachute jumping. Marriage? That's much more up my street. I had planned to ask you at Christmas, anyway; with perhaps an engagement of a year or so, so we can save up for the wedding."

Elizabeth leaned over and kissed him.

"I'm sorry if I jumped the gun, and took away your pleasure in asking me. But you know the answer is yes. It will always be yes. But why do we want to spend lots of money we can't afford, on a big, lavish wedding? I would be just as happy with a small, intimate wedding like today—just family and a few close friends."

"That suits me. So long as you and your Dad and my Dad turn up, I'll be happy. But what about your college course?"

"Oh, I still want to do that. But there's no reason why I can't go through college as a married woman, is there?"

"None at all. I just want you to be happy; for us both to be happy."

"Oh, I am. We will both be happy, I'm certain of that. By the way...I would still like to be proposed to in the traditional manner. It's just that you will already know what my response will be."

They fell asleep in each other's arms.

NEXT MORNING, as Elizabeth woke, she saw Dennis sitting on the end of the bed, holding a breakfast tray. She rubbed her sleepy eyes, and sat up.

"Breakfast in bed? Is it my birthday?"

He placed the tray on to the bed, leaned over and kissed her. Then she spotted the ring box sitting in the middle of the tray.

"Wow, I didn't expect you to be that quick."

Dennis went down on one knee beside the bed.

"We may as well do this properly."

He opened the ring box, containing the solitaire diamond that had been his mother's, and which his father had given him in anticipation of such a day. Taking the ring he held it poised to slip on to Elizabeth's finger.

"I love you, Elizabeth. I don't care if we only have one year together or fifty, but I can't imagine a life without you. Will you marry me?"

GRANT & JENNIFER

"THAT WAS A SWEET WEDDING, yesterday, wasn't it?"

They were chatting over a leisurely breakfast. Grant paused to butter his toast, before answering.

"It certainly was, and goes to show that you are never too old to marry."

Jennifer had an amused sparkle to her eyes.

"So, when you said you were putting me on notice, should I read anything into that?"

He grinned at her.

"Wait and see," was all he would say, mysteriously.

That was the only response she received from him, and realised he wasn't prepared to say anything yet. She would have to be patient. Of course, being a free, independent woman, there was no reason why she couldn't propose to him, but preferred to wait until he was good and ready. She knew her answer already. No doubt about it, but the answer was going to be yes.

She hadn't realised what was missing from her life until now. She had been quite content before he tracked her down again; she had had a great career, had beaten cancer, was loving her new writing career—but it wasn't until Grant came along again and slotted so easily into her life, that she appreciated what he brought; love, laughter and companionship; and of course, the sex, which she had missed. If all went well, they would be together for life now, she was sure. But the next move would be up to him.

OF COURSE, fate often strikes with a lethal weapon, when left to its own devices. Just a few weeks after their conversation, when Jennifer was alone in the house—Grant having gone to visit Lewis—the door bell rang. On the doorstep was a small woman, about mid-fifties, she thought.

"Hello, can I help you?"

"I hope you can. I'm looking for Grant Le Fevre. Is this where he lives?"

The woman had an American accent, and didn't look especially friendly.

"This is where he lives, yes. But he's not here at present. Would you like to leave a message for him?"

"And who are you?"

"I'm his partner."

Jennifer almost said 'wife', but decided that would be both presumptuous and untrue.

"So, you're not married to him then?"

Jennifer wanted to say, *mind your own darned business*, but decided against antagonising this woman. Still, she couldn't resist responding to the question.

"Not yet; but it's only a matter of time."

The woman laughed, derisively.

"Oh, really. Well you'd better remind him that he has a

wife—me. He will need to divorce me before he marries you, or else he will find himself in jail for bigamy."

She reached into her pocket and brought out a piece of paper, on which were scribbled some numbers.

"Here's my cell phone number. I'm over here for a week. If he doesn't contact me, tell him he will hear from my lawyer."

She stuffed the paper into Jennifer's hand, turned, and marched down the path; leaving Jennifer open-mouthed and in shock. Something like this had never entered her head. Grant had never once mentioned a wife, in all the years she had known him. Was this woman speaking the truth?

She went back to her writing, but couldn't concentrate, so began some cleaning in the kitchen; but all the time her brain was churning, as well as her stomach. It was two hours before Grant returned home, whistling as he came into the house. He heard the noise of pans rattling in the kitchen, and came to see what she was doing, tossing his car keys down on the work surface.

"No writing? Are you searching for fresh inspiration?"

"Not exactly. Searching for answers, actually."

Grant saw the grim expression on her face, and the smile faded from his.

"Are you okay? Nothing happened?"

Jennifer looked at him, signs of strain and sadness on her face.

"The simple answer is, no, and yes."

Grant walked towards her, intending to kiss her, or at least hold her, but, for the first time in their relationship, she backed away. He stood, arms open, as if hoping she would change her mind and run towards him. But Jennifer stood still, her face still grim.

"Your wife called this afternoon."

Grant's face turned pale.

"You mean, telephoned?"

"No, she came here, to the house, looking for you. I tell you, Grant, I am so hurt and confused. I don't think I can talk to you right now because I am so angry with you. I'm going for a short walk, and I want you to collect your things from the bedroom, and move into the spare room tonight. I need time and space to think."

Grant looked horrified.

"Jennifer, we must talk about this. It's not what you think. Please let me explain."

"Not now. I need some fresh air. I will be back in an hour. Here's her telephone number if you want to speak to her."

She handed him the piece of paper and grabbed her coat from the hook by the door, and moments later was gone.

GRANT NOTICED she had turned right at the gate, heading towards the park and the river. He sat at the kitchen table for a moment, his head in his hands. Just as everything seemed to be going well; then along comes something to wreck it. He almost felt like shedding a tear, but didn't.

He suspected Michelle might behave like this. It was just the sort of spontaneous, mad thing she would do. Should he have contacted her? Well, if he wanted to marry Jennifer, then he had no choice, did he? He had written to her, care of a mutual friend who he was sure would know how to contact her; explained his circumstances, and asked for a divorce. Until he was free, he couldn't propose to the woman he had come to love. Michelle was a mistake that took place a long time ago, and now, it seemed, he may have to pay the price of not dealing with it then.

With a heavy heart he went upstairs and did as Jennifer had asked; moving his stuff along the landing to the spare room. Taking some clean linen from the airing cupboard, he made up the bed, before sitting down on it and taking out his phone. With a feeling of dread, he pressed the buttons. His fingers were unsteady, and he had to press them twice more, before he managed the right combination. She answered in just a few seconds.

"Michelle?"

"Yes, Grant, your long-lost wife."

"When I wrote to you, I expected a letter in reply; maybe even a lawyer's letter; but not that you would turn up here. Where are you now?"

"About three miles away, at a motel on the route back to London. I have a car I rented at the airport."

"What do you want, Michelle, that couldn't have been dealt with by letter? It's not as though we were recently married, is it? How long ago was it? Must be nearly thirty years. The year we left college."

"Twenty-eight years to be precise, Grant. By the way, I call myself by my single name, Baker. I hated that fancy French name of yours. Couldn't wait to get rid of it."

"So you haven't wanted to marry again in all these years?"

"Nah! I just live with them, until I get bored, or they become mean and petty, and then I split. But you should know that, Grant. We were only together for six months, weren't we?"

"I didn't become petty; and I only became mean after I caught you in bed with my best friend from college. I should have divorced you there and then. I curse myself for leaving it all these years."

"Well, he was a bit of a loser. Kept having affairs, and dropped dead of a heart attack, while in bed with a woman he'd just met. I was glad to get rid of him."

Grant sighed.

"Why have you come, Michelle? We could have had this conversation via the phone from the US. I told you what you need to do with the paper I sent. Go to a lawyer and get it signed and then I can proceed with the divorce from over here."

"Well, I was rather hoping you had made a lot of money, Grant, and could afford to give me a lump sum as a divorce settlement. The last guy I was with stiffed me for all my savings. I've got nothing now. I need help to start a new life and to enable me to retire."

Grant laughed, sardonically.

"I thought as much. I knew there would be money mentioned at some point. Michelle, there is no earthly reason why I should give you any money. No court in either country would expect me to pay alimony after all these years. I assume you weren't pregnant when you left? If you had been, I would have heard about it, I'm sure; and, of course, I would have supported a child; but not you, Michelle. You're on your own, I'm afraid."

He heard the door shut downstairs. Jennifer must be back.

"I have to go, Michelle. I will call you tomorrow morning. Don't come back here."

. . .

JENNIFER TOOK OFF HER COAT, and went into the kitchen to make some coffee. She felt drained and depressed. The last thing she wanted right now was a conversation with Grant. When she heard him on the stairs, she picked up her coffee, and a couple of biscuits from the tin. They would do instead of dinner. She was in no mood to cook tonight. Grant would have to forage for himself.

She was about to leave the kitchen, when he entered—also looking tired, but she had little sympathy for him right now.

"I don't want to talk tonight, Grant. I'm going upstairs to watch TV in the bedroom. I'll pick up my laptop from the study too, in case I want to write tonight. I don't want any dinner. You help yourself to whatever you want. We can talk in the morning."

She walked past him and headed for the stairs.

"Jennifer…"

But she didn't pause, and carried on walking.

CHAPTER 14

$\mathcal{G}$RANT & LEWIS

JENNIFER AND GRANT didn't meet to talk things through the next day as planned. Early the following morning, Grant received a call from Doreen to say that Lewis's condition had deteriorated during the night, and could he come down.

Dressing quickly, and leaving a note for Jennifer, he drove quickly to Doreen's home. She greeted him, still in a dressing gown, and with a worried expression on her face.

"Thank you for coming, Grant. I didn't know what to do for the best. The nurse won't be here for another two hours. I wanted to call an ambulance, but Lewis expressly forbade me to."

She led the way into Lewis's room, where he was lying

down, his eyes closed. For a moment they thought he was gone, but his eyes flickered open, and he gave a weak smile at seeing Grant.

"So she's dragged you out, Mac, has she?"

Doreen fetched a chair so Grant could sit next to the bed.

"Would you like a tea or a coffee, Grant?"

"I'd love a cup of coffee, Doreen, if you don't mind?"

She bustled out of the room, looking relieved at having something practical to do.

"Well, buddy. How are you doing? Doreen seemed worried about you when she rang."

Lewis's voice was weak, but Grant could hear him clearly.

"Well, let's say I won't be going on any more patrols, Mac. I think my time is coming to an end. Thanks to you and Doreen, at least I won't be ending it all in a gutter somewhere; and I got to see my lovely Kristen again."

"Shall I send for her?"

"There's no time, Mac. I'm thinking hours rather than days. Tell you what, though, how about you record a little message for her on your phone? I'd like that."

"Yes, of course; anything you want."

He took out his phone and switched on the video facility.

"Okay, buddy, camera's ready."

"Prop me up a bit on the pillows, will you?"

Grant lifted Lewis forwards and pushed a couple of pillows behind his back. There was no need to comb his hair, for it was almost gone. His face looked bony and wasted, but there was nothing he could do about that. Doreen returned with his coffee, and the two of them helped him into a clean pyjama top.

"Wait a minute." Doreen bustled out of the room, and

returned a moment later with a small plastic purse, from which she extracted some make up. She deftly applied a little colour to Lewis's cheeks from a bottle of make up foundation—being careful to blend it in, and not apply too much to make it look too artificial. Grant agreed that it was an improvement; so as not to alarm Kristen too much.

Doreen left the room, rather than be a distraction and Grant began to film, holding the phone close enough to pick up Lewis's words. He began to talk.

"Hello Kristen. Don't be alarmed, but as you can see, I'm not too great. Please don't blame Mac for not telling you about my condition. He was acting on my orders, for a change. I knew, when we last met, that I didn't have much time left, but I wanted you to have happy memories of our time together, and not spend weeks sitting by my bedside, weeping. I'm afraid my life is nearly over, but I just wanted to tell you, honey, how much I love you and how proud I am of you. Since you were born, you have brought me nothing but joy. I remember feeding you with a bottle when you were just a few months old, and playing with you when you were growing up. Your Mom did an amazing job. And now you are all grown up and at college. Live your life fully and be happy, sweetheart. You will always be my sweet and precious little girl. I love you, Kristen."

He ended by blowing a kiss at the camera, and Grant stopped filming. They both watched it back together, to make sure it was satisfactory. Both men had tears in their eyes when it was over.

"Make sure she gets that, Mac. Probably when she comes over for the funeral."

The effort of making the video seemed to have tired

Lewis out, and Grant removed one of the pillows, so he could lie down again. His eyes closed as he began to doze. Grant sat by the bed, sipping his coffee—just being there for his friend.

Lewis never spoke again. By the time the nurse arrived, he had slipped into unconsciousness.

"It won't be long." The nurse agreed that he should remain at home, as per his wishes not to go into hospital.

At three-thirty-four that afternoon, Lewis stopped breathing, with Grant and Doreen sitting by his bed, and the nurse in the background. She did the vital checks and confirmed that he was gone. Doreen burst into tears, and Grant, feeling very tearful himself, hugged her as she cried.

"Thank you for what you did for him," whispered Grant.

"It was a pleasure. I came to care for him, even in the short time he was here. Thank you for being here for him too."

Grant knew there was one vital job he needed to do. To break the news to Kristen. It would be late morning in New York, and he didn't know if she would be in a lecture or not. But she answered quite quickly. As soon as she heard Grant's voice, she probably knew what the news was to be.

"Are you alone, Kristen? Where are you?"

"I'm in my room at college. My room-mate is here with me. Is it about Dad?"

Her voice was quiet.

"Yes, I'm afraid so. We lost him a short while ago. I'm so very sorry."

He could hear her weeping at the other end, but she was able to talk.

"Tell me about it? Was he in hospital?"

"No, he was at Doreen's. She and I were at his side when he passed. His last words were for you, Kristen. He asked me to record a message to you. Would you like to hear it? Or would you rather wait a while?"

She was silent for a moment, trying to control the tears.

"Not just yet, Grant. I'm not sure I can cope with it right now. I'll come over for the funeral, of course. Maybe you can give it to me then?"

"Of course. Will you be okay? I'll call you later on, shall I?"

"Yes, thank you, Grant. That would be good."

THE UNDERTAKERS ARRIVED to remove Lewis's body. There would be no need for an autopsy, because of his recent medical treatment, and a death certificate would be issued quite quickly, they said. Once that was received, plans for the funeral could be made.

The nurse gathered up the medical equipment and left. Grant gave a final hug to Doreen.

"Will you be okay on your own? Is there anyone you want me to contact?"

"No, there's no one to contact. I lost my only daughter, as you know. Lewis helped me a lot when he moved in. We both had a time when we thought the answer to life's traumas lay at the bottom of a bottle of alcohol. But he convinced me to stick to abstention, and I don't think I want to let him down now. I might go and talk to the vicar, Grace Bennett."

"Very well. I'd better go home and tell Jennifer what's

happened. I'll call again tomorrow and check on you, if that's alright with you?"

It was six-thirty by the time he finally arrived home. Throwing his keys on the kitchen table, he sank down on a chair, put his head in his arms and sobbed from pent up grief. Jennifer, alerted by the sound of the car and the door, came down and realised immediately what had happened. All thoughts of the events of the previous day went from her mind, as she went to the man she loved, to offer comfort in his sorrow.

GRANT & JENNIFER

GRANT AND JENNIFER lay exhausted on the bed, curled into each other's bodies. Yesterday and today had been traumatic, for different reasons. They had eaten a light supper and retired early to the bedroom. Grant related the events as they had happened that day.

"I sort of knew when I saw him that his time was to be measured in hours, rather than days. He looked so tired, and, in a way, ready to go. I was glad he was strong enough to record the message for Kristen."

"Have you saved it securely?"

"Yes, it's on my laptop now, too. Plus, I have put it on a flash drive to give to Kristen."

"What about the funeral?"

"As his next of kin, it will be up to Kristen of course, but I'll talk to her tomorrow, and let her know what Lewis told me. He asked for a church service here, followed by cremation, and for Kristen to take his ashes back to his childhood home. Of course, she has the right to make different choices, but I'm sure she will do what her father asked."

There was a pause for a few moments; both of them lost in thought. It was Grant who brought up the subject of the previous day.

"I'm so sorry I didn't tell you about Michelle. That was wrong of me. I thought if I contacted her and asked for a quick divorce, she would be obliging. But I had forgotten what a difficult woman she can be. To be honest, I have had so little contact with her over the years, I had almost forgotten she existed in my life. I want to tell you about her now, if I may?"

Jennifer didn't make any comment, but nodded her head solemnly.

"We were students together, and married as soon as we left college. As a girlfriend, she had been difficult at times, but after we married, I realised what a huge mistake I had made. She became temperamental and moody, and we rowed constantly. Then she became withdrawn, and I suspected she was having an affair with a friend of mine. I was right, and caught them together in our bed. It was so blatant and cruel. I told her to leave, and she went off with the man, who I had thought was a friend. Needless to say, he found out what a difficult woman she was, and they broke up about six months later. Michelle then tried to talk herself back into my life, but I wasn't about to make the same mistake again."

Grant paused for a moment, and looked down at Jennifer, to make sure he wasn't causing her any distress with his story. But she seemed calm, so he continued.

"I should have asked for a divorce there and then. But I

let it drift, and eventually I moved on with my life and virtually forgot she existed. It was only recently, after finally getting together with you, that I thought I should get a divorce and be free of her at last. I thought it would be a simple, straightforward process—but nothing involving Michelle is ever simple. I managed to track her down, with the aid of a mutual friend, and wrote to her, with a letter from a lawyer, asking her to agree to a simple, uncontested divorce. It would appear that Michelle, who has fallen on hard times, started seeing dollar signs in front of her eyes. Believing she could do better by meeting me face to face, she hopped on a plane and…you know the rest. I rang her and gave her hell over the phone and told her never to come here again, and that any communication should be through our lawyers. I'm hoping she got the message. I'm so sorry for hurting you. That was absolutely the last thing I wanted to do. Since being here all the time with you, I've come to realise that I love you dearly, and will do anything not to hurt you."

Jennifer raised her head and kissed him gently on the mouth.

"I have to admit, I was hurt and puzzled at first. I was sure I hadn't misjudged your character, and that I should listen to your story. But I'm glad you've come clean at last. But what will we do about her if she continues to cause trouble?"

"The lawyer I spoke to said that I would have no trouble getting an uncontested divorce, because of the length of time we were married, and subsequently been apart. He also said she has no right to any money from me. But I wonder if the simplest thing would be to give her a small sum of money to get rid of her."

"That may not be wise. Once she gets money from you, she may come back for more; like a blackmailer."

"But to get the money, she would have to sign a legally binding document that this is a one-off payment, with no admission on my part of any wrongdoing. Plus, she would have to sign the divorce papers. I can do that through the lawyers in New York, and we would have no further contact."

"Okay, if you think that's best. But as far as we are concerned, it is all over and done with. I trust you, and I know you to be a truthful and honourable man. I will support whatever decision you make."

They kissed, as though to seal the deal.

"I love you Jennifer. I didn't realise how much until recently."

The following morning, Grant spoke to Kristen on the phone, and they discussed the funeral of her father. She seemed happy to go along with whatever wishes he had conveyed to Grant.

"I'll make the arrangements with the vicar then. As soon as I have a suitable date, I'll call you and you can book a flight."

He went to call on Doreen, as promised, and related his conversation with Kristen.

"I need to go and see the vicar now. Would you like to come with me?"

"Yes, I would. I've spoken to her on the phone, so she's aware of Lewis's passing."

"Good. She'll probably need to speak to Kristen, but I

think we should try and fix a date, so Kristen can book the flight."

THE FUNERAL – THE REVEREND GRACE BENNETT

TEN DAYS LATER, thirty parishioners gathered in the pretty church, led by the Reverend Grace Bennett, and watched as the coffin, followed by Kristen and Grant, was carried down the aisle by the undertakers. On the top of the coffin was a wreath of white roses from Kristen, with the simple message 'To Dad, Love from Kristen' on the card. As a former US serviceman, he had been entitled to have the coffin covered with the flag of his home country, but had declined that honour, in his instructions. Instead, his medals lay on a blue cushion on the coffin. He had told Grant, "I fought for that flag, and was glad to do so, but I'm in another country now, and it doesn't seem right, somehow, to have what is a foreign flag to them on my coffin. It would have been different if the funeral had been in the US." Grant had been surprised how matter-of-factly Lewis had talked about his last wishes, as though it was a simple everyday event. But he seemed to have come to terms with what was about to happen.

Watching from the front, Grace saw the familiar faces of the people who had attended the wedding of Arthur and Dorinda a few weeks before. The newly marrieds held each other's hand throughout. Sitting with them were Dennis Mason and his now fiancée, Elizabeth, who both positively glowed with happiness, despite the fact that they were at a funeral. On the opposite side of the aisle, on the front row, sat Lewis's daughter, Kristen, who had flown in from the US two days earlier, with Doreen Trent on one side—trying, but failing not to sob—and Grant Le Fevre and Jennifer Blake on the other side. They looked solemn, but not overwrought as Doreen was. Grace knew she would have to keep an eye on Doreen over the coming weeks and months, to stop her slipping back into her old habits. Kristen was fairly composed, occasionally dabbing her eyes with a hanky.

Grace had visited Lewis two weeks before he died, and they had had a private hour when she had tried to offer him what comfort she could. The subject of their discussion, and its content, would remain private between the two of them, and not revealed to his friends and family. She was satisfied that he was at peace at the end, and ready to meet his Maker.

Seeing Grant and Jennifer, as well as Dennis and Elizabeth, she had no doubt that there would be more weddings in the not-too-distant future. In conversation with all these parishioners, in the short time she had known them, they reflected the joy and the sorrow that everyone had to go through as they travelled through life. None of them was immune to death and loss, but all of them had discovered the joy of love, of friendship, of loyalty, and community, that helped them share their hopes and fears that lay behind their closed doors. Sadly, there were people in the town whose doors remained firmly shut, and they were yet to find the answers we all seek as we travel through life. But Grace would do her best, in her new adopted community, to persuade more people to open the door to their homes and their hearts.

CHAPTER 15

$\mathcal{G}$RACE BENNETT & HANS WEISMANN

"Oh, darn it, no milk."

Grace was frustrated. It had been a long day, and she had set her mind on a cup of milky cocoa before bed. She glanced at the clock on the wall. Only nine p.m. The convenience store was open until ten. She would pop out and buy some.

The store was almost empty as she entered, except for an elderly man, slightly stooping, carrying a basket with several items in it. She would have spoken and smiled, but the man didn't look up. He seemed intent on his tasks.

By the time Grace had retrieved the carton of milk from the refrigerated cabinet, the man had reached the counter.

The shop-keeper, a turbaned Sikh, was scanning each item, and clearly knew the old man.

"How are you, Mr Weismann? I haven't seen you for a day or two."

The old man nodded and dropped his eyes again. He seemed a little shy to Grace, and she wondered who he was. It wasn't anyone she had encountered before. The man paid for his groceries, muttered a quiet thank you, and left the store.

Just seconds later, there was a crash, and a few young voices called out. Grace couldn't tell what was said, and moved towards the window to see what was happening. Outside, a group of young boys, six in total, probably aged around ten, stood in a circle around Mr Weismann, calling and jeering him. The crash had been from the newspaper advertising sign, which had fallen on to the ground – probably when the old man had staggered into it. Grace gasped, and her immediate reaction was to go to the old man's aid, but the shop-keeper beat her to it. Running out of the door he yelled at the young boys to clear off and leave the old man alone, or he would call the police. He led Mr Weismann back into the store.

"Are you alright?" she asked the man anxiously.

He looked up briefly, and nodded at her, probably noticing her clerical collar for the first time. She wanted to offer some practical help, so reached out to take his shopping bag.

"Let me help you home. This is heavy."

The man was about to protest, but looking into her kindly eyes, for the first time, changed his mind, and allowed her to take the bag.

"That's very kind of you," said the shopkeeper. "I'd take him myself, but I can't leave the shop unattended."

It was only a short walk to the man's rather shabby-looking house, that was desperately in need of a coat of paint. He opened the door for her, and she carried the bag into the kitchen and placed it on the table. He seemed out of breath, so Grace decided to stay for a few minutes.

"You sit down and catch your breath. I'll sit here with you for a few moments."

Mr Weismann sat gratefully down on to the kitchen chair. And Grace took the other one. She began to make conversation.

"I haven't seen you around here, Mr Weismann. How long have you lived in Swinbury?"

"My mother lived here since she arrived from Germany in 1942. I was here at first, before I went to London to study. I came back when I retired, to take care of her."

He seemed to surprise even himself with the length of his reply. Grace wondered how long it had been since he had had a conversation with anyone—a proper conversation. As a vicar, she came across a lot of lonely, old people—seemingly forgotten by the world. But then, she shouldn't make assumptions. Some people liked living a solitary life.

The old man still spoke with a strong, German accent, despite the years spent in England.

"May I ask how old you are?"

"I'm 87. I was ten years old when I came here."

"My goodness. You do very well, still looking after yourself at 87. Do you have any help?"

He looked at her blankly. The thought of asking for help had probably never occurred to him. Somehow, Grace having started a conversation with him, seemed to have switched something on inside him. He began to talk, in a soft, gentle voice.

"My father used all his savings to allow mother and me to escape from Germany. We're Jewish, and would have gone to the camps."

Grace drew breath, but said nothing; willing him to continue—which he did.

"He said he would try and follow us, but the Germans guarded him. He was a well-known scientist, and they needed his skills. But when they tried to force him to make weapons, he refused. So, they sent him to the camp. We never heard from him again."

"Oh, I'm so sorry." Grace's response was equally gentle and full of compassion.

"What did you do when you arrived here?"

"My mother had a cousin who lived in Swinbury, and she took us in, and I went to the school here. Then I went to University—Imperial College in London."

"How old were you when you went there?"

"Just sixteen. I was younger than the other students."

"You must have been bright."

"I suppose so. I never thought about it. My parents were very intelligent. I suppose I must have inherited it from them."

Grace was fascinated by his story now, and hoped he would tell her more.

"Tell me what happened after you graduated."

"They took me on as a research scientist, which I did for ten years. Eventually, after I gained my Doctorate, I became a

Professor, teaching students; which is where I stayed for the rest of my career."

"Then you retired and returned to Swinbury?"

"Yes. Mother had become frail, so I looked after her until she died. Since then I have lived here alone."

"It must have been lonely. How did you occupy yourself?"

The old man stood up, pulling on the table as he did so.

"Come through here. I'll show you."

He led her through to another room, which had bookshelves on three of the four walls, and a desk in the middle of the room. Piles of books were also on the floor. Grace had never seen so many books in a private home. She was surprised to see an old desktop computer on the desk. But then, with his time in academia, he would have been used to using a computer; at least in the latter part of his career.

He pointed to a row of books on the shelf closest to his desk. They all had the same author's name embossed on the leather spine of each book—Professor Hans Weismann, PhD. Grace could see from the titles that his science was Physics. He was clearly a very clever man, and now was living a solitary life in a small Oxfordshire town.

"You wrote all these? How wonderful."

"I haven't published anything for some years now. I don't keep up with the scientific progress so much now, since my retirement. But I'm pleased to say that my books are still used as teaching tools at the University."

"You must be very proud of your achievement, Professor Weismann."

The old man simply nodded his head and smiled. It was clear that he was gratified to be praised for his work, especially after such a long time. Grace felt sorrow that, after a momentous life, and great achievements, he should be living alone in obscurity, and facing the torment of ten-year-olds, who had no conception of who he was, and what he had endured when he was their ages.

"I know you are Jewish, Professor Weismann, but you would be most welcome to come along to our coffee club at the church. About twenty of the parishioners get together once a week for coffee and cake, and the chance of a conversation. You don't have to be Christian, or even religious at all, to attend. It's open to all. Eleven-thirty in the church hall every Sunday. Coffee and cake are free."

The old man looked gratified, and genuinely touched, by her invitation.

"Thank you. That is most kind."

As Grace took her leave, a plan was already being hatched in her mind. Doreen was grieving for her lost friend, Lewis, and had shown herself to be generous and kind. If she was willing, Grace would like to introduce her to Hans Weismann, in the hope that she would befriend the old man, and relieve some of his loneliness.

Reaching home, she realised that she had left the bottle of milk; the reason for her trip outside that night, on the counter in the shop. She was most gratified, however, when, on the following Sunday, as the men and women were chatting over their coffee and cake, the door to the church hall opened, and in came Hans Weismann, walking with a stick to aid his balance. He looked a little lost, and uncertain what to do. Grace went to greet him, but Doreen beat her to it, and led him to a vacant seat. Within minutes, he was chatting to people and sipping coffee; giving Grace a warm feeling that another lonely soul had been rescued from the shadows.

Just imagine if she hadn't decided to go for the milk that night. She shuddered at the thought and wondered how many other lonely souls were living behind closed doors.

TWO MORE WEDDINGS

AS WAS WIDELY PREDICTED, two more of these couples were to find their happy endings shortly after the funeral. A few days later, Dennis and Elizabeth went to see the vicar, to give her the happy news that they were to marry. Grace knew about the heartache Dennis had been through, in losing his teenage sweetheart, and the struggles of Elizabeth as she overcame her lifelong health struggle. They revealed their plans to marry as soon as possible, but also revealed a secret that Grace couldn't have imagined. They told her who had been the donor of the heart and lungs that had saved her life.

"My goodness. I had no idea. And you two had no idea too? It must have been a great shock when you found out. Does Doreen know?"

"No, not yet. We wanted to ask your advice. We wondered whether to tell her about it; especially now that she's lost her friend, Lewis. Maybe knowing the heart of her daughter, Charlotte, still beats in Elizabeth's body, might be of some comfort to her."

Grace gave the matter careful thought.

"This is a difficult conundrum. It will no doubt be a great shock to Doreen, and may revive some of the bad memories of her daughter's death. On the other hand, it may prove to be a great comfort to her, knowing that her daughter was able to give you a second chance of life. Would you mind if I gave the matter further thought, and perhaps talk to a psychologist about the possible repercussions to this. The young couple agreed.

A MONTH LATER, two weeks before their wedding, they gathered in Doreen's living room, with her and Grace, and primed with advice from the psychologist, and gently told her the truth about her daughter and Elizabeth. Doreen was stunned and hardly able to take it in. But slowly it dawned on her that a living part of her daughter was in the home where she had grown up. With tears running down her cheeks, she asked Elizabeth if she could listen to the heart, and Elizabeth agreed.

When, eventually, they came to leave Doreen's house, satisfied that she had accepted the news very well, Elizabeth reminded Doreen that both she and Dennis were motherless, and that they would be happy if she became a surrogate mother to them both. A new relationship, started in loss, but finishing in love, was born.

GRANT AND JENNIFER were not so quick to marry. It took a few strong letters flying back and forth between England and the United States, before Michelle accepted the sum of thirty thousand dollars for an immediate divorce, and no further contact with Grant and Jennifer. But eventually, it was agreed, and Grant took Jennifer to a local beauty spot where they loved to walk together. There, he went down on one knee and asked her to be his bride.

"I'm getting a bit geriatric to be getting down on one knee like this, but Jennifer Blake, the woman I was seeking all my life, and who I nearly let slip from under my nose, please do me the honour of becoming my wife."

She had to pull him up from his kneeling position, and both collapsed in a fit of giggles.

"Well, I was going to give you one more month, and then I planned to propose to you instead. But you saved me the indignity of kneeling on this wet grass. Yes, Grant, I love you very much, and I have no intention of letting you get away from me at any time in the future. You're stuck with me for life now."

As Grace conducted these last two weddings, she had a feeling of great satisfaction that despite the trials and tribulations of modern life, the human spirit was unquenchable and love usually prospered over hate. Lewis, who had suffered so much, had finally found peace, and the love of his daughter, Kristen. After tragic loss and a near-fatal illness, Dennis and Elizabeth had found a sweet love that she was sure would stand the test of time. Arthur and Dorinda had confronted Dorinda's past and Arthur loved her despite it. Doreen had finally come to terms with the loss of her daughter, Charlotte; and Hans had been rescued from his lonely world. Jennifer and Grant had ceased a lifetime of travelling the world, to find their worlds were, in fact, to be found in each other. It made Grace wonder how many untold stories were out there, behind closed doors, and hoped that they too might have happy endings. Maybe she too might one day find the love that these people had found. She just had to knock on the right closed door.

THE END

REVIEWS:

IF YOU HAVE ENJOYED this book, I would be so appreciative of a short review. It need only be a couple of lines, placed at the site where you purchased it, but will be of great help in getting the book some attention. Thank you.

ABOUT THE AUTHOR

Elizabeth Woolley is the pen name of a former English farmer, who enjoys the lovely English countryside, gardening, and travel. Unfortunately, the events of the past year have prevented the travel, but her writing has occupied her time instead. She hopes her characters are interesting and well-rounded, and that you think so too.

Elizabeth has a Facebook page (Elizabeth Woolley, Author) at

https://www.facebook.com/pg/ElizabethWoolleyAuthor

Printed in Poland
by Amazon Fulfillment
Poland Sp. z o.o., Wrocław